COM▍

Phyllis Kirks Crabb

8-1-2015

To Gene & Judy,

Dear friends and
neighbors, I hope you
enjoy the read. remember
1958 ...

Phyllis

Dog Ear Publishing
Indianapolis, Indiana

This book is a work of fiction. The characters, incidents, and dialogue are drawn from the author's imagination and are not to be construed as real. While a few actual place names have been used, any resemblance to actual events or persons, living or dead, is entirely coincidental.

First published by Dog Ear Publishing
4011 Vincennes Rd
Indianapolis, IN 46268
www.dogearpublishing.net

ISBN: 978-1-4575-3427-0

This book is printed on acid-free paper.

Printed in the United States of America

In Loving Memory of

ETHEL MARSHALL KIRKS

1925-2013

Chapter 1

No child should ever see what I saw that day. No child should ever feel the guilt that I felt. No child should have to keep the secret that I kept for as long as I did. I was almost twelve when the memory of that day started to bother me more frequently. I sometimes thought about it during the day. More often than not, I thought about it at night. Sometimes I dreamed bad dreams about it. Always in the back of my mind, I would wrestle with what God would want me to do.

All this turmoil started on a picture-postcard perfect Saturday in May of 1957. My daddy and older brother, Ben, had gone to a farm equipment auction in Charlotte, North Carolina. They left early in the morning, telling mama they would be gone all day, what with the long drive there and back. "If this old truck don't break down, we'll be back in time for supper," daddy said as he drove away. Trickem, the rowdy rascal of the neighborhood, was going with them in the old Ford pickup. I would like to have gone with them too, but mama wouldn't let me.

There was house cleaning to do before I could go anywhere. "A woman's work is never done," mama told me for the hundredth time as I swept the kitchen floor. She said after I finished dusting the furniture, I could spend the rest of the day with Latisha, my colored friend, who lived on a farm near ours. "Be home in time for supper!" mama called to me as I left. There was more cheerfulness in her voice than I had heard in a long time.

I walked over to Latisha's, about a mile down the hill from our house and through some woods. Latisha was with me when I asked her grandmother if it was OK if I stayed over there for a while. "Why shoo, Darla Mae. You know you is always welcome. But we's got to go to choir practice at three. You can stay 'till then," she said.

Latisha and I practically skipped down the path to the bold stream that ran through the back of their farm. Water rushed over the rocks, dropping several feet into a tiny pond that was surrounded by moss-covered boulders. It was an enchanting place, like something out of a story-book, the kind of place that tempted us to take off our socks and dangle our feet in the water, even when it was icy cold. On this day, we did just that, sitting on the edge of the biggest boulder. We talked. We laughed. We made up stories in a game we called "Truth or Lie."

At one point Latasha jumped into the little pond, scooped up a handful of water, and poured it over my head while saying, "I baptize you in the name of the Father, Son, and Holy Ghost." Her coffee cream face broke into a huge smile that showed off pearly white teeth.

"That's a lie!" I challenged her. "You aren't baptized until you are held under the water so you can be washed clean of all your sins," I said, repeating what I had heard in church all my life.

"It be the truth in my church!" Latisha's smile changed to a grimace as she pretended to be upset by my response. "We dunk and we sprinkle, depending on the time of year. If it be warm enough to take somebody into the creek, we baptize 'em there. If it be winter time, we just sprinkle 'em good." She giggled before saying, "You ought to join my church, Darla Mae. You could join in the winter time. Then you wouldn't have to worry about getting dunked."

"Oh yeah, I could do that... when pigs fly! Can't you hear the congregation whispering, 'What dat white gull be doing in our church?" I watched Latisha's hazel eyes roll to and fro while she thought about how her church members would deal with a little white girl in their midst. Both of us got caught up in describing how other people, colored and white, might react if I was to join a colored church. She mimicked a prissy white lady pinching her nose and saying I smelled bad because I hung around colored people. We exaggerated accents and words, laughing until our sides ached.

Finally Latisha said, "Seriously, Darla Mae, you know you need to go ahead and join one of those churches you go to. It's what all the kids our age are doing. You might as well do what everybody else is doing. Don't even think about it. Just do it!"

The hours passed quickly when I was with my friend. Long before I was ready to leave, it was time for me to go home. I declined the offer of a ride, preferring to take my time getting back to the house where my mama was sure to find some more work for me to do.

When I was in sight of the house, I noticed a strange car in the driveway. "Mama must have a visitor. Maybe it's one of those vacuum cleaner salesmen who had been going through our community this week," I thought. Not wanting to get dragged into helping him show how one of those things worked, I went in the back door, closed it quietly, and tiptoed into the kitchen. That's when I heard faint noises coming from my parents' bedroom.

That perfectly beautiful day was spoiled instantly by the sight of my mama in bed with a man. Both of them were naked. They were squirming around, grunting and groaning, doing gross and disgusting things with each other. Arms and legs all twisted and tangled. Mama's long strawberry-blonde curls covered enough of his face that I couldn't tell who he was. I knew he wasn't my daddy.

I watched, wondering what I should do. Scream? Yell at them to stop? Leave before they saw me standing in the doorway? My heart was about to beat right out of my chest. When my stomach started to churn, I knew I had to get out of the house as quickly and quietly as I could.

Once outside, I stopped long enough to throw up, before running to the treehouse daddy had built for Ben and me. In spite of my age, I was still small enough and short enough to sit in this space that had offered comfort to me on many occasions. Ben and I would often come here when we had been scolded or whipped for some mistake we had made.

Kati, my calico cat, was curled on an old blanket in the corner. She stood, stretched, and walked over to nuzzle my legs. I picked her up, petted her, and felt grateful for her presence. "I hate her," I told Kati, who sniffed my breath and swiped at the tears that started to run down my face. "What am I going to do?" I asked aloud. "If I tell her what I saw, she will probably kill me. Kill me deader than a door knob! If I tell daddy, he will probably kill her. Then he'll be hauled off to jail and I'll be an orphan. What am I going to do?"

Kati curled up in my lap, laid her head on my leg, and closed her eyes. She had no answers.

Neither did I.

Chapter 2

When I heard the man's car leave, I waited a little longer before I headed home. Mama was listening to the radio, singing along with some old country song when I came into the house. She bustled around the kitchen, preparing food with unusual cheerfulness. I wondered how long this mood was going to last.

"You're home earlier than I expected," she said when I came through the back door. "Didn't you and Latisha have a good time?"

Mama never cared whether I had a good time!

"Oh, uhh… yeah, we always have fun together." I couldn't look her in the eye.

"What did y'all do?" mama asked as she uncovered the bowl of dough that had been rising on the kitchen counter all afternoon.

Part of me wanted to ask "What did *you* do all afternoon? Who was that man in here with you?" I knew better than to ask.

"Latisha sprinkled me with water and said I was baptized. Said I had been washed of my sins."

"Humph! Y'all don't know nothing about sin. And there ain't no reason for you or anybody else to be baptized when they're too young to know what they're doing." She made a fist and punched down the raised dough so hard I thought she was going to smash right through the bowl.

Daddy got home a short time later, gave her a quick hug, and commented on how pretty she looked. Mama was a pretty woman with sky blue eyes that had been sparkling ever since I got home. She seemed to be on fire from within.

My brain was on fire too, wondering and worrying about what I should say or do. I tried to write in my diary that night, but could only manage three words. "I saw mama…!" That was enough to force me to find a new place for my diary. I hid it in the false bottom of my sock drawer, hoping that no one would ever discover it.

That night and for many nights afterward, I'd close my eyes and see mama and that man, naked and all wound up together. Then I'd dream a bad dream. By the summer of 1958, I knew I had to do something to make the dreams stop. But what? Would joining a church, getting baptized, confessing my sins make any difference? But what sins? Was seeing what I saw and not telling anybody about it a sin? I wrestled with these questions almost every night before finally falling asleep.

Chapter 3

*F*lames leap from an enormous pit somewhere in the distance, far away. People are moving toward the pit, some being dragged to it, their naked bodies bruised and bleeding. Their screams and cries for help echo off the mountains nearby.

Others run toward the pit, as if eager to cast their lot with people who are already there. Suddenly I am being drawn toward that pit as well. A force that I cannot see is pulling me as I try to kick it away. Both of my arms extend away from my body. The force is exerting pressure on my left while a white-gloved hand grabs my right wrist, drawing me back. A featureless face vanishes amid the crowd's laughter—the high-pitched, grating, hideous sort of laughter that I have heard from witches in Halloween costumes.

The white-gloved hand is pulling me into a tunnel that is straight and narrow, becoming even more restrictive as I travel further into its depths. I am suffocating. Kicking and screaming, "Leave me alone," I try to free myself. My left arm becomes detached, but then springs back, just as the same hand clamps down on me again. Horrified, writhing in pain, I scream.

Mama gripped my shoulder and shook me hard, calling my name, "Darla Mae, Darla Mae, wake up!" The urgency in her voice pierced my deep sleep, but only momentarily.

"Huh?" I groaned and rolled away from her, wondering if I was dreaming that my mama was really here in my bedroom in the middle of the night.

"Darla Mae, wake up!" she yelled again, shaking me even harder. The box springs of my old four-poster bed squeaked. "What is wrong with you?" she demanded to know. Her voice was almost panicky as she pulled the white sheet and homemade quilt off me.

"Huh?" I grunted, reaching for the sheet.

"Sit up and answer me!" mama insisted as she lifted my head off the old feather pillow.

"What?" I asked, trying to open my eyes. They felt like they had weights on the lids, holding them shut. Finally a slit of moonlight appeared. It filtered through tattered lace curtains, hand-me-downs from Grandma Deacons, and outlined my mother, all five feet two inches of her slender figure, staring down at me. A wild tumble of curly hair fell across her face and her long white night gown shimmered in the moonlight, making her look like a ghost.

"You must have been dreaming—having a nightmare," mama said. "You've been moaning and groaning so loud that the dogs got to barking outside."

I listened for a minute. Two old hound dogs that lived on our farm were howling like they'd encountered a stranger. I could hear daddy talking, but couldn't understand what he was saying.

"Dogs barking?" I wondered what that had to do with me.

"Your daddy has gone out with the shotgun to see who is out there. He thought maybe somebody's trying to steal something—the car or tractor—or maybe Trickem is out there drunk and acting crazy. You know how he is."

"Yeah, I know how Trickem is. He's a devilish drunk sometimes." I said.

"I don't like your daddy being out there with a loaded gun. Somebody is likely to get shot."

"Daddy… out with a gun?" I asked, still trying to make sense of why mama was in my room if they had heard something going on outside.

"I told him the noise was coming from your room. It was, too. When I walked in here, you were kicking and groaning and carrying on. What on earth have you been dreaming?" she asked again, taking a seat on my bed.

"Wasn't. Wasn't dreaming," I muttered, not sure at that moment if I had been dreaming or not. What difference did it make, I wondered. I was awake now.

"Well, you must have been. You've been making enough racket to wake up the dead." Mama leaned closer to me as if she wanted to see if I was awake or just talking in my sleep. I could smell her breath. Onions from last night's supper.

"Awake now," I said, trying to look her in the eye.

"Well? What were you dreaming?" she asked again, stroking my arm with her calloused right hand, the one with the deformed thumb. I could feel the multiple ridges of that thumb as it gently caressed my forearm. Mama often rubbed our arms when she was upset about something. I think it helped her to calm down. My brain was activated now, searching its memory cells for clues to a vanished dream.

10

"I don't remember." I said, trying to sound honest.

Mama could almost always tell when I was lying. She said my whiney voice and twitching chin were dead give-aways.

From my parents' room downstairs the wail of my frightened baby brother interrupted my mother's interrogation. I could have kissed "Bug," my baby brother. He had a way of demanding attention that simply could not be ignored.

"Well, go back to sleep then. I hope you don't have any more bad dreams tonight." Mama kissed me lightly on the forehead, a rare maternal gesture of affection. She started to close the door, then stuck her head back in the room.

"Remember, we have to get up early tomorrow. We're going to Cousin Charley's church and to his house for dinner."

I slid back down on my pillow and searched for a comfortable spot on the lumpy old mattress that had out worn its useful life long before it was put on my bed. I pulled the covers up around my shoulders and lay there thinking about my bad dreams.

There had been several of them recently, with each one becoming more frightening. They usually came on the nights after I had been to church. A red-headed woman was usually in my dreams. There was always a fire. Someone was always talking of sin, of sinners, and hell.

I was afraid that I might go there someday. To hell, that is.

Now that I was almost twelve years old, I was thinking a lot about sin. About sins I had already committed. About sinful things I had seen.

Most of my friends had recently joined a church, been baptized, and promised to live a righteous life. Not me. I had not been "saved." Nor had I "joined" a church. Not that I hadn't had my opportunities. I just hadn't done it yet, nor was I sure that I wanted to.

Daddy told me to wait until I was old enough to know what I was doing. "It's not like joining a 4-H Club or any other club, for that matter. It involves *serious* commitment." He'd usually leave the room before mama could start her lecture on how he ought to get baptized himself.

As far as I knew, daddy had never made that *serious* commitment, even though he was now almost forty-one years old. He said he felt close to God every day as he plowed the fields, tended the crops, and cared for the animals on our fifty-acre farm. Daddy said he believed in Jesus as his personal savior, even prayed when he felt the need, but he knew there was a lot going on in churches that wasn't what God wanted; therefore, he was better off not belonging to one.

Mama had come to her decision late in life, about two summers before, in fact. She was thirty-two when she walked down the red-carpeted aisle to the altar of Healing Waters Gospel Church while the congregation sang "Just As I Am." Tears had streamed down her face as she walked slowly, hesitantly toward the altar where Preacher Harold Hardshell took her by both hands and asked her to kneel beside the other two women who had come forward to make a profession of faith.

I remember that night, sitting in the white weatherboarded country church amid the smells of yesterday's Pine Sol scrubbing and today's mixture of baby powder, perfume, aftershave, and lilacs. Preacher Hardshell shouted and pounded on the pulpit throughout the sermon, telling us all what a sorry bunch of sinners we were. He stood way up there on the top level of the altar, all six feet four inches of him, side by side with the life-size painting of Christ. I wondered why our preachers always wore nice suits, white shirts, neckties, and shiny shoes when Christ was always painted wearing a flowing beige robe and sandals. Shouldn't our preachers look humble, like Christ? I was always wondering about something like that, especially when the sermons got boring.

Reverend Hardshell looked movie star handsome with his wavy black hair combed away from his tanned face. He had perfectly straight white teeth and a smile that could light up a room. His intense brown eyes, however, appeared to blaze with fury as he continued his sermon.

Several people in the congregation agreed with him, saying "Amen" out loud when Reverend Hardshell talked about the wickedness of young people today. "Dancers, drinkers, and fornicators." He said, "They are all going to hell."

"God is ashamed of you and you and you!" he shouted, pointing at several people in the sanctuary. He pointed right at mama.

I knew mama wasn't a dancer. She wasn't a drinker, either. Maybe she was a fornicator, but I didn't know what that word meant. (I thought I'd look that one up when I got back to school, where there was a big dictionary with thousands of words in it, but I just kept forgetting to do it. Besides, I didn't want anyone to know that I was curious about something sinful.)

"God knows your sins!" Reverend Hardshell's booming voice vibrated off the windowpanes.

"God knows your sins!" he repeated, lowering his voice, hanging his head and stepping away from the pulpit for a moment. He stopped, looked sideways, and seemed to stare right at me. Could he have known what I was thinking?

"You will burn, burn, burn in hell for all eternity if you don't repent of your sins now." His voice got louder with each "burn." I squirmed on the hard wooden pew and thought about that fire in hell being fueled with wood. If so, everybody going there would smell like wood smoke, like our clothes always smelled all winter. Maybe we were already in hell and just didn't know it.

The good reverend had hit the podium with a thunderous rap of his fist. I thought he was going to smash it to smithereens, right then and there. I wish he had. It would have served him right for trying to scare the dickens out of us. I would have laughed out loud.

Mama answered his altar call that night and got baptized six months later. Along with a couple of other people who had joined church about the same time, mama attended confirmation classes at least one night a week. Sometimes she had to go twice in one week when the preacher thought the converts needed more instruction on some aspect of the Bible. Mama never missed a class. In fact, she seemed to look forward to the sessions.

❦

Always one to try to look her best whenever she went out in public, Mama had curled her long, thick hair on pink sponge rollers the night before the baptism. The next morning she combed out the curls, powdered her face, put on a light pink lipstick, and wore her best Sunday dress, a bright blue cotton shirtwaist that she'd made especially for the occasion. I thought she looked awfully pretty.

On the day of the baptism, our family went down to the creek with mama and a whole slew of relatives to watch the proceedings. A person getting her life right with God was a cause for celebration, witnessed by as many family members and community folks as could find a place to park along the dirt road leading to Little Creek. There must have been about a hundred or more people gathered around the place that locals referred to as Holy Pond, since it was the deepest and widest body of water on this side of Pittsylvania County and was always used by the local churches for baptisms.

"It sure is hot here today," I said, pushing my bangs off my face, as we drove to the creek.

"Darn good thing!" daddy said. "I remember a time when the preacher had to break ice to dunk old man Jessup. At least your mama will dry out fast." He grinned and playfully slapped at mama's hand.

We found standing room near the creek bank in the shade of a gigantic birch tree whose thirsty roots ran deep into the bottom of Little Creek. A light breeze filtered through its dense leaves, bringing up the musty odor of decaying matter in the thicket nearby.

Reverend Hardshell opened the service with a prayer, followed by a few words about the reason for the day's baptism. He introduced the converts and asked them if they repented of their sins. Mama said, "I do," just as the other two ladies had done.

One by one, Reverend Hardshell led them into water up to his waist. Mama stood motionless, staring at the preacher as he baptized the other women. When it was mama's turn, Reverend Hardshell took her by the right hand and stepped back into the water. I could tell she was holding onto his hand for dear life. Mama was afraid of drowning; she never got into water that was over her ankles. I watched wide-eyed as Reverend Hardshell pinched her nose and said, "I baptize you in the name of the Father, Son, and Holy Spirit." Then he dunked her in the muddy water to wash away her sins, holding her under water for what seemed to me to be a long time before she opened her eyes and came up sputtering, looking a whole lot like a drowned rat we'd found in a bucket out by the barn.

Usually starched, crisp, and clean, Reverend Hardshell's clothes now looked like they had soaked up all the filthy sins of the new converts. He dried his hands on a small towel before reading from Romans, Chapter 6, in the King James Version of the Bible. Then he had us join in singing "We Shall Gather at the River." Afterwards everyone was invited to come forward to welcome the new Christians to the fold of Healing Waters Gospel Church.

Like everyone else, I went forward to shake hands with the three women. Actually, I hugged mama the best I could, without getting myself wet. As I watched the other people offering their words of welcome, I wondered if I'd ever stand in the same place, free of sin, a person recognized as "righteous" in the eyes of God and man.

When I said as much to my older brother, Ben, he snickered. "Not anytime soon, Sis."

On the way home, I asked mama "Why did Reverend Hardshell hold you under the water for so long? Did he think you had accumulated a lot of sins?"

Mama blushed and laughed. "Why that's just the way preachers do it, Darla Mae. You'll see, it's not so long, when you get baptized someday."

Daddy rolled his eyes and mumbled, "Humph."

Still, I wondered.

I couldn't see that her baptizing made any difference in how mama behaved. I wondered if it was supposed to make a difference. I wondered if I got baptized now, before I had a chance to commit any major sins, if the preacher would maybe just sprinkle some water over my head like I'd heard folks do in other churches. Like the Methodists do. That would suit me better than being dunked in muddy creek water, since I don't know how to swim and don't rightly know what I'd do if the preacher accidentally dropped me.

Lying there thinking about sin was keeping me awake. However, if I went back to sleep, I might have another bad dream. Goodness knows I didn't want to wake up my parents again. I surely didn't want to wake up those mangy old hounds, nor any of the dead that occupied the two cemeteries on the family farm.

I could hear my older brother, Ben, loudly snoring through the door that connected his bedroom to mine. At twelve, going on thirteen, that boy (whose short height, slender build, mousey brown hair, and aqua eyes matched mine enough to look like my twin) could sleep through an earthquake. I thought maybe I would go in there and sleep with him for the rest of the night, but realized I couldn't do that. Mama wouldn't like it. She had said many years ago that we were too old to sleep together like we did when we were little kids. That's when she put both of us upstairs in separate rooms.

I had been happy to get my own room, even if it meant that I had to sleep where there was no heat in the wintertime. Even though the sheet rock in the room had been up so long without paint that it had turned a deep brown color. Even though the ceiling sloped so that a person over five feet tall couldn't stand up straight on two sides of the room. Even though the only closet was once a packing crate for a refrigerator. Even though I had to go through Ben's room to get to mine. Even though I had to use a chamber pot since there was no bathroom in the house. Mama often said that some folks were so poor they didn't have a pot to pee in. That made them even poorer than us.

Still, I loved having my own special space where I could go to read undisturbed while my mind traveled to exotic places, where I could write in my diary, where I could fantasize about the good life and beautiful home that I would have someday when I was grown.

My dream house would have two stories with big white columns, a front porch with a swing, and would be surrounded by several acres of lush, green grass. There would be tall, perfectly shaped trees around it—magnolias, maples, dogwoods, and pines. I'd have some azaleas and lilacs, and roses, too. I'd even grow some honeysuckle on a fence out back, just so I could enjoy its sweet fragrance in the spring. When nobody was looking, I'd suck some syrup right out of the blooms.

There wouldn't be any stables or pigpens or chicken houses nearby. No yucky smells. No messes in sight of the house. Nothing but beauty would surround my home.

I'd sleep in a big, brass bed in a room where pink and yellow roses bloomed all year long on my wallpaper. There'd be great big closets—enormous closets, big enough to walk right into them, and a kitchen with all electric appliances. No more toting in wood, filling up wood boxes, and sweeping bark off the floor several times a day. And it would have a bathroom, maybe two or three of them, where I could soak in a tub of clean, hot water with bubbles floating all around me. Bubbles... floating... all...around....

My eyelids grew heavy and my mind relaxed, no longer worried about sin and eternal damnation. The next day our family was going to the Holy Bible Believers' Church, where Cousin Charley was the minister, and to his house for midday dinner afterwards. We would commit the sin of gluttony, and who knows what else.

Chapter 4

The smells of sausage frying and biscuits baking woke me up. I quickly dressed in an old pair of green pedal pushers and a yellow button-up shirt before I skipped down the steps and ran barefoot through grass still damp with dew, down the hill to the outhouse.

Our outhouse was a deluxe edition, a two-seater that was well-ventilated due to the way it had been built with green wood planks, which dried and shrank in oppressive summer heat, leaving gaps between them about a half-inch wide. Apple, peach, and cherry trees nearby, along with a couple of huge oaks in the back yard, channeled a breeze through these cracks most of the time, keeping the inside air fresh and occasionally fragrant.

Mama and I kept it spotlessly clean, sweeping the wood floor and scrubbing the porcelain seats (a set that daddy had picked up somewhere) once a week with hot water and Pine Sol. We replaced the tissue when needed and made sure that the Sears, Roebuck and Montgomery Ward catalogues were always available for anyone who might want to pick out something to buy while they were doing whatever they came to do. On this particular morning I took care of my basic needs and hurried back to the house.

"Wash your hands," mama reminded me before asking, "Did you sleep OK the rest of the night?"

"Yes, ma'am. I went back to sleep not long after you left my room." I thought that statement was close enough to the truth to keep my chin from twitching. As I drew cold water from the white enamel kitchen sink, one of the three modern conveniences that we had, I thought about the date—August, 1958. The way my family lived, this could have been 1858.

"Well good," she said as she searched in the refrigerator for something. "Did you remember to gather the eggs yesterday?"

"I think so," I lied, remembering that I hadn't fed the chickens either.

"No you didn't! Now get down to the hen house and see if you can find some for breakfast." She slammed the door of the refrigerator. "There aren't any in here. I used up all that we had on hand yesterday morning for the cakes, deviled eggs, and potato salad."

Mama turned her attention to straining the milk that daddy had brought in from the morning's milking. The two of them had been up ever since the sun peeked over the pasture to the east, the same as every other day of the week. Ben was at the pigpen with a bucket of slop, taking care of two hogs that were being fattened for slaughter in the fall. Daddy had gone to the barn where he stoked the fire under the latest curing of tobacco.

I grabbed an egg basket and headed back down the hill to the hen house, a weatherboarded building with a large white door and a pole that ran from the ground up to a miniature door that was just big enough for the chickens to go in and out. Inside I gathered six eggs from wooden boxes lined with straw, being extra careful where I put my hands and feet. Chickens are really bad about leaving their droppings everywhere.

"When I grow up, I'm just going to buy my eggs from the grocery store," I thought. "And I'll certainly never kill and pluck another chicken if I can help it."

The day before, mama had chopped the head off of an old hen that she wanted to use for chicken and dumplings. She'd held it by the feet and removed its head with one swift blow on the chopping block. That old hen fell off the block and started flapping around, spewing blood all over the place. It flapped and rolled with mama chasing it all the way down the hill, through the hay field to the pigpen.

Mama chasing that chicken was a sight to behold. Her red print housedress was blowing in the breeze. Her arms were flapping and her hands were opening and closing, trying so hard to grab that chicken, it looked like they were going to dance with each other. A chicken dance—arms flapping, hands grabbing, wings flapping, and bodies shaking. Ben and I tried to mimic those moves and about fell over laughing.

"Daddy, do I have to help you eviscerate this ole hen?" I had asked, hoping I could be excused from this unpleasant task.

"Eviscerate?" Daddy looked at me like I had spoken a foreign language. "What in tar-nation is *eviscerate*?"

"That's one of those vocabulary words Mrs. Rivers taught us last year. It means the same thing as "gut" but I think it sounds a lot better. Don't you?"

"I sure do, Darla Mae. That's a fact. I'll try to remember that the next time I need to clean the entrails out of some animal." Daddy grinned, a gap-toothed sideways grin, which told me that he was proud of me. "Mrs. Rivers said you were one of the smartest students that she'd ever taught. She said you had finished the sixth grade reader and knew all the vocabulary words after the third week of school. Said you done real well on some kinda test. Scored at the twelfth grade level on your reading, too. I guess it's time for you to teach your ole pa some things. What else did you learn that might be useful on the farm?"

"Just a minute, I'll remember something," I told him. Then my mind took a turn the way it often did, recalling something that had been said or done in the past.

Mrs. Rivers had grown up in MacKenzie, knew most of our parents, and had taught many of them, which had given her plenty of exposure to the way we talked. She told us we should always speak respectfully to our parents, using words they would understand and being careful of how we used words, especially verbs. "Remember—I see you now; I saw you yesterday, and I have seen you many times in the past. Never. Never. Never say *'I seen you.'* This was one of her pet peeves and soon became one of mine.

"Daddy, Mrs. Rivers told us some easy ways to remember the right words to use, whether we are on the farm or someplace else. For instance, she said, '*Ants* have four legs and crawl on the ground. *Aunts* have two legs, walk upright, and are the sisters of your parents. *Ain't* has no legs because there isn't any such word. Isn't she one of the smartest people we know? Besides you, of course!" I watched a pleased smile play over daddy's face. As much as

I loved him, I really wanted to be more like Mrs. Rivers, in every way possible.

"Think and write using your expanded vocabulary," Mrs. Rivers had said. I really enjoyed the challenge of thinking and writing at a level above what I heard in my everyday life. Listening to different dialects and translating what was being said into correct English was a game I played in my head.

Daddy had asked me a question that I wanted to answer more completely, so I thought about how Mrs. Rivers had taught us how to determine the possible meaning of a new word by breaking it into familiar parts. After a moment's thought, I said "Odorous. The *-ous* at the end of a word means a lot of something, so when you add it to odor it means an abundant amount of unpleasant odor. That's a word that applies to lot of stinky situations on the farm."

Daddy laughed as he dunked the hen into boiling hot water and started to remove the feathers. "It sure applies to this one!"

I felt so sorry for that poor ole hen I wanted to cry. "Daddy, do you think it is right for people to kill animals and eat them? After all, the Bible says, "Thou shalt not kill.""

"Well, Darla Mae, a person can question a lot in this crazy old world, but when it comes right down to people being able to live, eating animals is one of the ways people have to feed themselves. I happen to think that is why God put them on this earth in the first place—to be a source of food for other animals and for us humans. Do you remember in the Bible where God had his people bring animals to be slaughtered and used as burnt offerings?"

I nodded and mumbled "Uh-huh."

Daddy continued, "Well, based on that, I think it's OK for a man to feed his family with anything God has provided."

"I guess so," I said, still feeling bad about that poor ole hen. "I just don't like to be on a first name basis with my food. When I grow up I want to buy it all in a grocery store."

Being out there with daddy, talking so compatibly, gave me the courage to bring up the questions that had been troubling me for over a year now. "Daddy, there is something I have been wanting to ask you about," I began. Furrows formed a question mark between his raised eyebrows. I hesitated, debating with myself over just how much I wanted to share with him. Even though it had been a long time since I had seen mama with that man, I thought it was news that daddy would not want to hear, so I posed a question that Mrs. Rivers would have called "hypothetical."

"Daddy, if you saw somebody do something that you thought was wrong, like cheating on a test or throwing a rock through somebody's window, what would you do about it?"

"Darla Mae, has Ben done something I need to know about?" Daddy stopped picking the feathers off that ole hen and stared at me.

"No. No. Not Ben. This has nothing to do with Ben. I was just wondering what you would do. Would you talk to the person who was doing it, or would you tell someone else about it who might do something about it? Or would you just forget about it, if you could?"

Daddy twisted the hen around where he could get to the side I'd been working on. He mulled over my question for a couple of moments before answering. "Well, as a general rule, I'd say you need to let the person who was involved know you saw him. But before you go accusing someone of doing something wrong, you need to be sure that what you thought you saw was what was really going on. You also need to ask yourself some questions, like who am I going to help and who am I going to hurt if I tell what I saw? Who is going to be hurt if I do nothing? Does that make sense to you?"

"Yeah, I guess so."

"Are you going to tell me what it is that you are really concerned about?" Daddy's eyes met mine, an expectant look encouraging me to give a detailed answer.

Before I could launch into the secret that I'd been keeping for so long, mama yelled out the back door. "Darla Mae, come take care of Bug so I can help your daddy get that hen ready to cook. It'll never be done in time for supper if we don't get it ready soon."

I gladly left the unpleasant task, but felt frustrated that I hadn't been able to tell daddy what was really on my mind. Perhaps there would be another opportunity to share the secret with him soon. I sure hoped so!

Back at the house I washed the eggs and broke them into a bowl. Mama added milk, salt, and pepper before pouring them into a skillet of hot grease. They sizzled and coagulated into a soft yellow mass. In no time at all, our breakfast was on the table.

Daddy took his usual spot at the end of our red Formica-top kitchen table next to the back door while mama sat in a red vinyl chair at the opposite end next to the wood cook stove. Ben was on the side next to the Kelvinator refrigerator and I was next to the sink. Doug the Bug, my baby brother, sat on mama's lap while she gave him tiny bits of table food that he might be able to eat. On this day he drank from his bottle and ate some of the gravy from last night's dumplings. Anybody could see why mama stayed so thin. She hardly ever had a chance to eat.

"Y'all chaps need to finish your breakfast and get cleaned up to go to Cousin Charley's church this morning," daddy reminded us, his mouth still half full of food.

I wanted to tell him that "chaps" were something that cowboys wore over their pants when they were riding horses, but that would have been disrespectful. Daddy would have slapped me in the mouth for sassing him. Then he would have told us for the hundredth time that he didn't have the opportunities that Ben and I have had to go to school. Grandpa Deacons had made him quit school when he finished the seventh grade so that he could help with the tobacco crops. "Growing 'bacca is a thirteen-month-a-year job," according to Grandpa.

Mama only got through grade school, too. Even though mama wanted to go on to high school and nursing school, her parents needed her to help on the farm and with the younger children. Her pa said, "Girls don't need no education to rock a cradle."

All of daddy's dreams about becoming a medical doctor and mama's dreams about becoming a nurse ended when they were only a year older than I am now. Thinking about that made me sad. I knew that I could never correct daddy or mama, no matter how bad their grammar was, no matter how incorrectly they used the English language.

That didn't stop me from thinking about the right way to say things, though. I often found myself correcting them in my head, and I made a point of trying to be correct in how I used language so that I would grow up talking pretty, the way my teachers did.

"Mama, is it all right if I wear my new green dress, the one you made for me to wear for the maypole dance? If I decide to join church today, I can look good walking down the aisle." I flashed a cocky smile that I knew would get a quick response.

"You can wear whatever you want, but you are not joining Cousin Charley's church today or any day. Nor any other church, for that matter." Mama glared at me as she said that.

"Why not?" I asked, knowing that I could be in big trouble any minute.

"Because I said so." Mama had standard replies for many situations, and this was one of them.

"You are not old enough. You don't know what you are doing," daddy chimed in. I could feel him glaring at me the way he often did when he didn't want any argument.

"But all my friends are joining churches and getting baptized." I ate the last bite of my eggs and spread strawberry preserves on the remainder of my biscuit, making sure that I didn't make eye contact with daddy. If he only knew the secret I had kept for well over a year now. If he only knew what had caused my bad dream last night. What would he want me to do?

"If all your friends were jumping off a cliff, would you jump off a cliff, too?" daddy asked.

"No, she wouldn't! She's scared of heights," Ben said, speaking before I could even find a good reason for saying that I would do whatever my friends were doing, before I could blurt out my other big reason for wanting to get baptized.

"What if I wanted to join at Healing Waters?" I asked.

"Those people wouldn't want you in their church." Ben picked up his plate and slid behind daddy and me to put it in the sink.

"Humph! A lot of room you have to talk. Your sorry soul hasn't been saved either," I reminded him as I took my plate to the sink where I scraped my leftover sausage into a tin pie plate we used to feed Kati and the dogs.

"Yeah, but I'm not a thief either," Ben teased me with his flashing aqua eyes and exaggerated smirk.

"Neither am I!"

"You are, too."

Ben's accusation stung me more than he could possibly have realized.

"Am not," I crossed my arms over my chest and double-dog dared him to call me a thief again.

"That's enough out of both of you," daddy stood up and clenched his fists, adding the authority of his six-foot tall muscular frame to his words.

I knew it was time to shut up, wash the dishes, and get cleaned up as daddy had ordered. Walter Deacons was usually a sweet, soft-spoken man, but there was a limit to his patience. He would not tolerate conflict of any kind. When he got angry, his eyes would meet yours and burn holes right through to your brain.

With wash-pan and soap in hand, I climbed the narrow, enclosed stairs to my room to get cleaned up and dressed for church. Being called a thief had really made me mad. Ben knew that. He didn't have to bring it up. I wondered if there was a book of rules somewhere that said an older brother's job was to irritate his younger sister by repeatedly reminding her of her mistakes, sounding a lot like a broken needle on a 45 r.p.m. record.

Chapter 5

I was only about seven years old when I became a thief. Mama had taken me with her to Russell's Store where we did most of our tradin.' That's what folks around MacKenzie called shopping. Russell's Store was also where we went for some fun.

Located on Highway 41 just south of Swansonville, it was well-stocked with ice cream that Mrs. Russell scooped right out of five-gallon containers, soda pop of every flavor, penny candy including Mary Janes, Tootsie Rolls, and licorice sticks. Of course, there were bags of coffee, sugar, flour, sliced bread, and rounds of hoop cheese. The store even had nails, hog feed, fence wire, and all sorts of stuff that farmers might need.

There was a pot-bellied wood stove on the left side of the store, which radiated its heat all around the place during the cold winter months. A small wooden table with lots of nicks, gouges, and cigarette burns, was a favorite gathering spot. A man could buy a bottle of grape Nehi, a chunk of cheese, a pack of crackers, and then grab a seat in one of the straight-back chairs while he played "set back" or poker or some such card games with the locals. Ashtrays were plentiful, since many of the farmers smoked cigarettes that they rolled themselves using little white squares of tissue paper and crushed bits of tobacco they'd cured themselves.

I hated the smoke that hung in the air in this and every other little country store around Danville. It turned the walls a sickening beige color—what part you could see for all the merchandise that was piled up on display and hanging from the ceiling, that is. Worst of all, cigarette smoke stunk, just like my clothes after I had been around it for a while. It made me cough and wheeze, too. I knew I didn't want anything to do with tobacco when I grew up—not growing it, and definitely not smoking it.

Most of the local women didn't seem to mind the smoke, or maybe they just didn't want to admit it if they did. If they came along with their husbands to do some shopping, they could sit on the other side of the stove, chatting with their neighbors. Who was sick, who was having a baby, who died, who was putting in a quilt, who canned the most snap beans... that was the usual talk around that side of the stove.

Mrs. Russell would occasionally ask them to go out to her house to see something new she had made from one of the bolts of fabric that was also sold in her store. Meanwhile, the kids would play checkers or some other board game on the floor. Sometimes one of my girlfriends and I would go into the back of the store where we could sit on the bags of hog feed while we talked and "smoked" our candy cigarettes.

On the day of the theft, mama and I had gone to the store to pick up some sugar and jar lids that she needed for canning pear preserves. Mrs. Russell took mama to the back of the store to show her a new bolt of Dan River fabric that she thought mama would like. Meanwhile, I wandered around the floor and looked at the merchandise, stopping in front of a couple of bushel baskets of apples: one red delicious and one golden delicious.

I picked up a little red one, just big enough to fit in the palm of my hand. I stood there looking at it for several minutes, thinking how good this apple would taste. My mouth started to water as I thought about how it would crunch as I bit into it, how it would squirt out a fine mist of juice as my big front teeth pierced its thin red skin, and how I would roll that pulp over and over in my mouth before swallowing it for a final burst of sweetness. No wonder these apples were called *delicious*.

I knew better than to tell mama that I wanted some of these apples. She would respond with her often repeated statement, "Want horns and die butt-headed." I simply have not figured out what this meant, except "no, not now, and probably never."

My older brother and I had been taught early on that we must not ask for anything. Daddy would answer our request with "You are old enough that your wants won't hurt you." The truth was that sometimes they did hurt.

I walked over to the ice cream box to see if there were any new flavors when I heard mama and Mrs. Russell come back to the front of the store. As soon as mama paid for her purchases, we left. We were almost home when I noticed the little red apple was still in my right hand. Mama noticed it, too, almost instantly.

"Darla Mae, where did you get that apple?" Mama's voice and face were stone cold.

"Mr. Russell gave it to me." I felt my chin twitch, the way it always did when I was telling a lie.

"Mr. Russell wasn't even in the store today." Mama stopped the car in its usual bare spot in our yard and turned to confront me face-to-face. "You stole that apple!" mama yelled at me. "How dare you! How dare you embarrass all of us by stealing one little bitty apple!"

If looks could have killed me, I'd be too dead to be telling this story right now. Mama's eyes were firing off rounds faster than my daddy could fire his pistol. Nothing, and I do mean nothing, was worse than embarrassing our family by what we did and what we said. I looked down at the floorboard, feeling more shame than I could ever remember.

"You sit here while I go tell your daddy. And don't you dare eat that apple," mama ordered as she got out of the car and headed to the big barn where daddy was working on his tractor.

I watched her walk briskly, her anger evident in every step, until she disappeared through the side door of the barn. Any minute she would probably reappear with daddy and a switch and I'd get a good whipping for sure, I thought. At least I'd still have this juicy delicious apple.

Sitting there staring at the little apple, I remembered the story of Adam and Eve. Hadn't God asked them not to eat the apple? Eve was tempted to eat it anyway, by a snake, which was really the Devil, causing Adam and her to be thrown out of the Garden of Eden forever. I closed my eyes but quickly opened them again when a huge black snake slithered through my mind. Suddenly, my little apple didn't look so tasty. It was an evil thing that had tempted me to steal.

I let the apple fall to the floorboard where it rolled under my seat. It was out of my sight now, but I knew I had to retrieve it before mama came back, so I slid off the blue vinyl seat and onto the floor. I had just pulled it out when I heard mama and daddy's footsteps crunching on the gravel driveway behind the car. Sweat beads were breaking out all over my face and I was starting to tremble as I climbed back into my seat.

"For Pete's sake, Darla Mae! What in the world made you do such a thing?" Daddy's voice was seething with fury. "As if I don't have enough to do around here without having to deal with you stealing something. An apple, of all damn things! Do you know how embarrassing that is for this family? Makes us look like we don't feed y'all. Why didn't you just ask for the apple if you wanted it? We may be poor; but we are not so poor that you young'uns have to start stealing food. Besides, we've got damn apple trees right here in the yard. Couldn't you have got one right off the tree?"

I knew better than to interrupt him while he was ranting like this, so I just sat there with my head down, holding onto that stinking little apple. Daddy went on asking questions that he didn't want me to answer, sometimes leaning into the open window next to me, sometimes backing away from the car and shaking his fists. Finally, he finished the tongue-lashing and fell silent for what seemed like several minutes. I looked at him wipe sweat from his forehead with a shop rag before putting his ball cap back on his almost bald head.

"I'm sorry, daddy. I won't do it again. I promise." My voice was soft and low, but still loud enough to ensure that daddy heard me.

He gave me another one of those brain-penetrating looks. "I've got to get back to work. Your mama can deal with you now." With that said, he strode off back to the barn, kicking up dust and gravel with his worn out clod-hoppers.

I turned to face mama, who had been standing by silently while daddy ranted and raved. She uncrossed her arms, planted her hands firmly on her hips, and looked me straight in the eye.

"Darla Mae, me and your daddy talked about this and we think the thing to do is to take you and the apple back to Mrs. Russell. You have to hand it to her and tell her that you stole it. She can punish you any way she wants to. If she wants to give you a whipping, she can." Mama walked around the car and slid into the driver's seat.

I sat there in silence, trying to imagine how I was going to tell sweet Mrs. Russell that I was a thief, that I had stolen an apple. Would she allow me to come into her store again? Ever? I started to cry. This was worse than a whipping.

When we got to the store, mama gave me a handker-chief to clean my face before I went in to see Mrs. Russell. Mama walked behind me as I clutched the apple, feeling its woody stem.

"Mrs. Russell, Darla Mae has something she needs to tell you," mama said to the lady, whose round face and big brown eyes registered surprise at seeing us again so soon.

Mrs. Russell knelt in front of me, nearly face-to-face. I held out my fist and opened it. "I… I… I sto…le this app… apple when we were here this morning," I stuttered, trying really hard not to start crying again. "I'm real… really sorry and I prom… promise never to steal anything ever again."

She must have seen I was about to cry, because she took the apple from me and said, really kind and gentle-like, "Thank you, Darla Mae. You did the right thing, bringing it right back to me."

"I told her that you could punish her any way you want to." Mama's voice was still angry.

"Am I gonna to get a whipping?" I asked.

"No, I am not going to whip you," Mrs. Russell said softly, a broad smile forming on her sweet round face. "Your mama probably won't whip you either." She looked up at mama and shook her head. "I think bringing the apple back and confessing to me is punishment enough." She gently patted me on the back.

Mama was standing there with her arms crossed over her chest, looking mad as a cat being given a bath. "I ain't raising our young'uns to be thieves."

"Oh, I know you're not. Darla Mae is not a thief. I expect she just forgot that she had picked it up. Children are always picking up stuff here in the store. We usually notice before they get out the door." She stood up and looked mama in the eye. "It's alright now, Alene. It really is."

On the way home I told mama, "I'm never going to steal anything ever again as long as I live." It had been almost five years, and I'd kept my word.

Now, if only I could get Ben to keep his big mouth shut, my life would be much happier. I really wanted to tell Ben about what I had seen the year before, but I didn't think I could trust him, not the way he kept bringing up this incident with the stolen apple. If he only knew what I knew, he'd never mention that apple again.

Chapter 6

After loading the car, an ugly green wood-paneled 1949 Ford Dream Wagon, our family finally climbed in to make the fifteen mile trip to Cousin Charley's church. Daddy said that it didn't matter where we were going; we still took everything with us except the kitchen sink.

That seemed to be the case since Douglas Wade Deacons (Doug the Bug) was born. We had to take food, diapers, and toys, along with several changes of clothing for him, as well as extra clothing for us. The little bugger got car sick about every time we went anywhere and threw up all over us. Sometimes we just hung his head out the window and let him upchuck while we drove on to wherever we were going. Mama believed in being prepared for any emergencies so we had towels and wet wash clothes in plastic bags, just in case we needed them. Today we were also taking a devils' food cake and a peach cobbler for dessert. Those goodies were in the back, safely away from Bug.

On the way we passed Bethel AME Church where Uncle Travis Mitchell had been buried the Friday before. There was a green tent still covering his grave, stamped with the name of the local colored funeral home, announcing the recent death to all the living who passed by. Red clay piled up around the edges of the grave created a frame for numerous colorful flower arrangements, which had started to fade in the August heat. I looked toward the gravesite for a couple of seconds, then looked away and bit my lower lip to keep from crying.

Uncle Travis was not my real uncle. He couldn't be because he was colored and much older than my parents' brothers. He and Aunt Essie (not my real aunt, either) lived on a small farm near ours. They had been there forever, probably since before my daddy was a baby. Now they had grown old, but were still very active as they raised two grandchildren—J.R. and Latisha Banks.

Uncle Travis had died suddenly of a heart attack. After mama and daddy got word, they talked about whether they would go to the funeral. They had plenty of time to decide since Uncle Travis' relatives had to drive in from places like Detroit and New York, where several of their children had gone to get jobs and make a better living for themselves.

"You know people will talk about us if we go," mama had said. "They'll be calling us..." she looked at me and apparently chose not to say the "n" word. "Well, you know what they'll be calling us."

"Don't care if they do," daddy countered. "Colored folks' blood bleeds red, just like yours and mine. They ain't no different under that skin."

"Yeah, I know. But the other neighbors will talk if they hear we went to his funeral."

"Well, why don't you just ask some of the other neighbors who has helped them with their 'bacca crops for the past forty years? Do you remember what he did when I broke my right arm during tobacco planting season?"

Mama stopped what she was doing, held the measuring cup full of sugar over the mixing bowl, and looked at daddy with glistening eyes. "Yeah, I most certainly do. That good man came over here and planted the whole five acres. I can see him now using that old hand planter while I dropped the plants and you carried water with your left arm. If it hadn't been for his help, we might not have had a crop that year."

"And remember the time when all of us were down with the flu? Uncle Travis and Aunt Essie were the first people in the neighborhood to bring food and help with the chores."

Daddy nodded his head as he chewed on his bottom lip, trying to keep his emotions in check. Finally he spoke again. "I'm going to miss all those evenings sitting out here under these big oak trees playing our guitars together. That man taught me how to make those guitar strings sing the blues."

"And you taught him how to play some white country music, too. Bluegrass. Gospel. Y'all made some good music. I always enjoyed listening to you playing together." Mama's words seemed to lighten the moment a bit.

Daddy inhaled a deep noisy breath before declaring, "*I* am going to the funeral. You and the young'uns can come with me or you can stay home."

"Well, I wouldn't feel right about not being there. Not paying my respects," mama let the metal spoon that she was using to mix cake batter slide down into the bowl with a thud before she gave daddy a sympathetic look. He put his arms around her and they cried together.

Hearing their discussion was too much for me. I quickly decided to forego the opportunity to sop the mixing bowl. Never mind that I loved anything made with chocolate. Instead I headed outside, letting the screen door slam on my way out to our tree house in the woods. Tucked between two old oak trees, the treehouse offered a place where I could be alone to think about things.

There I sat with my head on my knees and cried for a little while until Kati climbed the stairs, stood on her hind legs, and bumped my head, her way of telling me to sit up so that she could get in my lap. Once settled, she started to purr ever so softly. How did she know that I really needed her company?

I loved Aunt Essie and Uncle Travis as if they were my blood kin. They had always been a part of my life, playing with me and teasing me when I was very young. Uncle Travis had always called me "Little Gull."

When J.R. and Latisha came to live with them, I asked mama why they were here. She said, "That's not anything you need to know, so don't be asking anybody about it again." She looked at me with tight lips and squinted eyes, the way she always did when she meant what she said.

"But why are they here?" I asked again, really curious now that she didn't want to tell me.

Mama said, "It is nobody's business but theirs. Now promise me you won't ever ask any of them about it." Complying with mama's wishes made my life easier so I kept my wondering to myself.

Soon Aunt Essie brought the grandchildren over to meet us. J.R. was a tall teenager with light brown skin, sparkly brown eyes, and pretty white teeth. Daddy hired him to help with planting and harvesting the tobacco crops. He said that J.R. was smart as a whip and could make a dog laugh. He just had a habit of finding something funny to say about everything. The fact that farmers could depend on him to show up on time and do a good job made him popular with all the folks in the area. Daddy said "If something needs to be done, J.R. will go ahead and do it, without being asked. In my book, that makes him the best help for miles around MacKenzie."

His little sister, Latisha, was almost a year older than me, but we were in the same grade in school. She came to play with me whenever Aunt Essie came to visit my mother or to help her with putting in a quilt or something like that.

At first Latisha was shy about playing with me. Later she told me that she was scared of honkeys. I asked her what a honkey was and she said "That's you, whitey! You's a honkey." My face must have reflected my lack of comprehension because she went on to explain, "I's a nigga. You's a honkey." Latisha giggled and shook her head, jostling red, orange, and yellow ribbons that secured little plaits all over her head, making her look like someone had plowed rows through her kinky reddish-brown hair.

"Oh," I said, shocked to hear her say the "n" word out loud because mama and daddy had told us never to use that word. In fact, I got one of the worst whippings of my life for saying that word when all I did was to ask for some "nigga toes" while one of mama's colored friends was helping her make apple cider. My question had embarrassed mama and shocked her friend. It had also shown my ignorance.

Between licks with a forsythia limb that left welts on my legs, mama had said, "What you wanted was a Brazil nut. The "n" word is used for someone who is sorry, low-down, no-account and good-for-nothing. It's a cuss word.

I don't want to ever hear you using that word again. Do you hear me?"

Remembering this incident, I had to ask Latisha, "Does that mean I, Darla Mae Deacons, am a really bad person?"

"Naw," Latisha drawled, her thin angular face, the color of creamed coffee, tilted to the right, "You's not bad." Her mischievous hazel eyes caught mine as she shook her head of colorful ribbons again before changing the subject, "Did you know that white people smell like milk?"

"Milk?" I frowned at her, my big nose all scrunched up like I smelled something rotten. "You know I hate white milk. You can't pay me to drink it unless you add some vanilla flavoring and lots of snow in the winter time to make snow ice cream." Saliva formed in my mouth just thinking about that sweet white treat. "And in the summertime, if you add some syrup made with sugar and cocoa, that is a different story. If I smell like milk, it has to be *chocolate* milk!" Both of us laughed silly schoolgirl laughs until our sides ached.

Latisha and I spent our time talking, playing, and picking blackberries from the vines that grew on the edge of our farm. Both of us loved school, loved music, loved to dance, hated tobacco, and wanted to leave MacKenzie when we grew up.

One day she complained about the long bus ride to her school, which was all the way over on the other side of Chatham, about twenty miles away. "Why don't you and J.R. just go to school at MacKenzie?" I asked her. "Our school has all twelve grades in one building and it is only about six miles from here. You could catch the bus with Ben and me."

43

Latisha hung her head and spent a few moments thinking before she answered. "You're gonna have to "ax" your mama to 'splain that one to you." Then she looked at me sad-eyed, like my question really hurt her.

When I asked my mama about Latisha and J.R. going to the MacKenzie School, she said that colored people and white people couldn't go the same school.

I asked "Why not?"

Mama said, "Because that's the way it is." She didn't even look at me, but kept right on shelling peas.

"But why is it that way?" I asked again.

"Because that's the way it's always been. Coloreds know their place and we know ours. They've got their schools, their churches, their bathrooms, their water fountains and we've got ours. Coloreds and whites don't mix."

"But we do mix here at home. Latisha and I play together. Ben and J.R. work together. Why can't we mix at school?" I wanted to know the real reason for sending us to separate schools.

"Darla Mae, if coloreds and whites go to school together, they might start datin' and marryin.' Then they'd be having little high-yellow babies, little mixed race babies that nobody would claim. Now you just put those questions out of your mind. Life is the way it is because God meant for it to be that way."

Mama's explanation left me frustrated. I wrote about it in my diary that night.

It can't be God's will for life to be unjust. No matter what mama says. No matter what people have always done. Aren't we all His children? Surely He would want everybody, colored and white, to have a good education. Wouldn't He? If I had my way about it, Latisha and J.R. would be riding the bus with me, going to my school!

Those conversations ran through my mind as I watched people come into the church for Uncle Travis' funeral. Elderly colored men shuffled in, leaning on home-made wooden canes. Buxom young colored women sashayed down the aisles in stylish, tight-fitting black dresses trimmed with white collars. They must have been from New York or somewhere like that because their clothes looked like they were made from silk or some fabric that you couldn't buy around here. One woman had a pretty round face, a short curly haircut, and full red lips that matched her red and black plaid dress. She was about twenty years old and she wobbled when she walked, probably because the heels on her shoes were so high. You could tell she wasn't used to wearing them.

All of the men, young and old, wore dark suits with stiffly starched white shirts and narrow, striped ties. Many of them, especially the local farmers, had peeled off their jackets and were fanning themselves with their felt hats. Sweat beaded on their foreheads and left large wet rings under their armpits. Overweight middle-aged women waddled in wearing navy and black print dresses with jeweled necklines and pleated skirts that covered their bare legs to just below the knee. It was much too hot for stockings. Hats of all shapes, sizes, and colors complemented their snazzy outfits. I think Uncle Travis would have been right proud of how his family and friends dressed up for his funeral.

He'd usually worn bib overalls and plaid shirts around the farm, but on Sunday he'd always dressed in a dark brown suit, white shirt, and brown tie with little green and yellow stripes running through it. Often he'd laugh at himself, using one of his favorite expressions, "I cleans up right good when I goes to church, like I's gonna look when I's laid out. I wants the Lawd to recognize *me* when I gets to the pearly gates. Yeah, Lawd, he gonna know me when I gets there!"

I'd been to several funerals before this one: my grandfather's when I was five, my grandmother's when I was seven, and several older relatives that I didn't even know the year before. They were all white funerals. This one was different because almost everybody was colored, except for my family and one other neighbor's family.

Folks in the church looked at us strangely, especially when we went up to the front of the church to view the body. I had seen some of the people touching Uncle Travis when they looked at him, but I knew I didn't want to do that. Touching dead people was creepy. I didn't even want to go up there to look at him, but I was a little bit afraid to sit in the back pew with my baby brother while everybody else went to take a last look.

The five of us slowly moved down the red-carpeted aisle toward the altar that was surrounded with more flower arrangements than I could easily count. Mama always wanted to know how many flower arrangements there were at a funeral. She said you could tell how well respected the dead person was by how many of them people had sent. The scent of roses, carnations, and gladiolus was almost overpowering in a sanctuary filled with them. Sunlight streaming through stained glass windows cast blue, green, and red shadows across everybody and everything, making the whole church look like something from another world.

Uncle Travis was laid out in a shiny, metal coffin with a silky-looking white liner. His face was old and wrinkled like it had always been, unlike my grandma who had cotton balls or something stuffed in her cheeks when she died so that her skin was soft and smooth as a baby's tail. Uncle Travis' gray hair was almost white, which made his ebony face seem even darker. Daddy had always said Uncle Travis was *pure* black, whatever that meant.

Taking a quick look, I turned to follow my parents back down the aisle, but they had stopped to speak to family members on the front row. I spotted Latisha sitting beside Aunt Essie and waited my turn to hug her while mama, daddy, and Ben spoke to Aunt Essie and J.R.

"He sure looks natural," mama said as she hugged Aunt Essie.

"'Sho 'nuff do. Natural 'nuff to speak." Aunt Essie dabbed her eyes with a handkerchief, edged in lace and blue embroidery.

"We're really gonna miss him." Daddy took Aunt Essie's hand and gave it a squeeze while putting a piece of "green" in it. I couldn't tell if it was a one, five, or ten dollar bill. "If you need anything, anything at all, you let us know."

She nodded her head and whispered, "Thank you, Mr. Walter."

I noticed that Aunt Essie's extra-large vinyl handbag was open on the pew. It had more bills showing on the top than we usually see in the collection plate at Cousin Charley's church on a Sunday morning.

There were other people waiting behind us and I didn't know what to say, so I just told Latisha that I really liked her grandpa. She looked at me with eyes filled with tears ready to trickle down her cheeks any minute. "Thank you for coming here, Darla Mae." Then she leaned closer and whispered, "You not a honkey at all. You my true friend." I didn't know what else to say, so I hugged her again and walked away.

I had started back down the aisle when someone called my daddy's name. "Mr. Walter, you and yo' family sit down right here." He pointed to a pew that was only about five rows back from Aunt Essie. The colored man, whose face I had seen but whose name I didn't know, slid over to make room for all of us. I knew from the other funerals I'd been to that the closest family occupies the first row and as many other rows as are needed to accommodate them. What did it mean that we had been asked to sit so close to the front? We certainly weren't "family," but maybe they thought of us as extended family. If that was the case, that would be all right with me, since Latisha was definitely like a sister.

Settling back into my seat, I was feeling awfully sad about Uncle Travis, but good about the friendship that I had with Latisha. Perhaps this friendship was part of my redemption, my salvation. Maybe I wasn't such a sinful person after all. (At least I wasn't a honkey!) The Bible tells us to love our neighbors as ourselves. Does it say anywhere in there that our neighbors have to look like us or talk like us or even think like us? I figured I'd have to read more of the Bible to be sure, but I couldn't imagine that Jesus would have told us not to love someone because her skin was a different color than ours.

Lost in my own thoughts, I missed the opening words of the service, but soon got caught up in shouts of "Hallelujah" and some old-time gospel singing. "Swing low, sweet chariot, coming for to carry me home..." That choir was all decked out in shimmering blue robes, like the color of the sky, only darker blue, with white satin collars. Their voices loud, strong, and clear were singing in a style that I'd never heard. They were clapping and swaying and some of them were singing one verse while others sang different words. If the Lord wanted people to make a joyful noise, I'd say the folks at Bethel AME were doing just what the Lord wanted.

Fascinated, I started to rock from one hip to the other with the music, as I noticed other folks around me doing. Those old oak pew benches creaked with the shifting weight of all of us, but they could barely be heard for all the sobbing and mournful sounds that were coming from the front rows of the church. There was a group of women sitting in front of us who had been crying, moaning and carrying on since they first walked into the church. You would have thought they had practiced how to mourn: their sobs and wails were so powerful. Just listening to them made me want to cry.

The preacher started talking about Uncle Travis. "This good man is heaven-bound because he was saved long ago and has lived a righteous life, serving the Lord."

"Hallelujah!"

"Praise the Lawd!"

Shouts came from several folks around the church. I sort of tuned out here and there, choosing instead to look at the hymnal to see if colored folks sang any of the same songs as white folks. They did. I also found that AME stood for African Methodist Episcopal, something I'd been wondering about for a long time. Then I started wondering what they believed and if they had any strange ideas about what people ought to wear or do. I wondered what they'd say about what I'd seen my mama doing!

Occasionally the preacher's voice would roar and thunder, bringing me back to what he was saying—something about eternal life if we were "saved." Then he would whisper some words so softly that I had no idea what he was saying. He thundered again, "I urge you, brothers and sisters, if you haven't been saved, see me after the service so that you, too, can walk the streets of gold with Uncle Travis someday."

I wondered if I could talk with him about how getting saved might help me. I really needed to tell somebody about my bad dreams and what I'd seen that was keeping me awake at night. I started to listen to him again, more focused than I had ever been in church.

"Tell me now, do you want to see Brother Travis in the next life?" The preacher raised his right hand and looked around the congregation.

"Yeah, Lawd!" a few people shouted, holding both arms above their heads.

"I ask you again, do you want to walk the streets of gold with Brother Travis in the next life?"

"Yeah, Lawd!" It sounded like everybody shouted out this response. My daddy even said, "Yes indeed" out loud. Now, in a white church, we don't usually speak out like that. We usually just sit quietly listening to what the preacher says. Sometimes I would count the number of pews and calculate how many people were at the funeral so that I could tell mama when we got home. She likes to know that sort of thing. On this day, I tried hard to pay attention to the preacher.

I could hear Aunt Essie sobbing while the preacher continued what he called his celebration of Uncle Travis's entry into heaven.

"Travis was a good man…"

Several people shouted "Yeah Lawd!" and "Hallelujah!" including a man who sat behind me.

"A man who truly loved God with all his heart, soul, and mind… a man who truly loved his neighbor as himself." The preacher walked around to the front of the podium.

Loud shouts of "Yeah, brother" came from the family pews.

"You only have to look around you to know that Travis was faithful to this commandment." The preacher stopped and searched the congregation with eyes so piercing that I thought he could see right into our hearts.

"Hallelujah!" "Yeah, brother," and a few "Amens" could be heard in the congregation.

Suddenly Aunt Essie let out a wail so long, so loud, so pitiful that it seemed to carry the force of a raging storm. That cry ascended all the way to the rafters where it rumbled around, before its pain rained down on us, drenching us in sorrow. I'll *never* ever forget that sound.

Men blew their noses. Purses snapped open as women searched for handkerchiefs. Even mama and daddy busily blotted tears away from their eyes. I caught Ben's eye just as huge tears fell. Both of us sniffled and reached for our handkerchiefs. Mercifully, Bug was sleeping through all of this.

After what seemed like an awfully long time, white-gloved undertakers ceremoniously closed the lid on Uncle

Travis's coffin and rolled him out of the church and on out to the cemetery. All of the family followed him out there, then the pews emptied from front to back, so we were among the first to leave the church. Some folks nodded a greeting to my parents as we walked past them. I sensed their respect and felt proud of my family for being there.

I didn't want any part of that scary hole in the ground, though, so I went to the car with Ben while the graveside service was going on. We took Bug with us, since he needed a diaper change. I laid him on the car seat and pinned a dry diaper on him while Ben fiddled with the dial on his little transistor radio. Since my stomach was growling, I was eager to get home where I could get something to eat. I wanted to change into shorts and spend some time playing with Kati. Petting her always helped to cheer me up. Unsaved soul that I was, I felt sad and confused, all mixed up about the right and wrong of things in my life. That colored preacher had got me to thinking that I needed to get my life right with God. Right now. If I ever wanted to go to heaven. If I ever wanted to tell someone what I had seen.

Chapter 7

Daddy jolted me right out of my reverie when he slammed on the brakes. He started honking the horn in short beeps just as we rounded a curve near the church. I slid forward, banging my knees against the back of mama's seat. It didn't hurt much, but I immediately wondered if someone could make a strap or something to hold a body in place when a driver had to stop suddenly. When I hit the back of her seat, mama had to grab the dash board with one hand, while holding Bug tight with the other to keep him from flying out of her open window. His loud screams let us know that he was more frightened than any of us.

Ben had slid forward and bumped his head on the car doorframe. There was a small red spot, but he was too hardheaded for a little encounter like that to do any serious damage. He was now leaning out the window on his side of the car. Sitting on the edge of my seat, I could see now what all the commotion was about.

"Dang cows! Where do you suppose they came from?" daddy wondered aloud as we all stared at the five black and white Holsteins ambling along in front of us, taking up both lanes of State Route 57. One particularly dirty bull turned to face the car, forcing daddy to come to a complete stop. He bellowed and then dropped his head with his horns pointed toward us like he was going to charge our car. This ugly bull took a few steps toward the left side of the car, where he stopped, stretched his neck toward our open windows, and lowed long and loudly. We could smell his breath, a sickening odor of digested green grass and wild onions. Ben and I exchanged looks of disgust, but I knew that he was just as excited by this encounter with the cattle as I was. This would give us something else to talk about after church.

Daddy honked the horn a few more times before pulling off on the shoulder and opening the door of our old station wagon. I knew that daddy didn't want to chase those cattle back to their pasture, wherever that was, but there was little else he could do.

"Now, Walter, don't you get out there and get yourself dirty," mama cautioned. She turned to look at Ben and me. "Y'all stay in the car. 'Em cows could be mean. That ugly bull right there looks like he wants to attack somebody."

Mama didn't have to worry about either of us messing with the cows. We were smart enough to know that cows have great big heads and little bitty brains. That's why they get out of a lush green pasture to look for food on the other side of a fence, although the other side may be an asphalt roadway. They don't seem to remember if you are a friend or an enemy. Dumb cattle. Except for ole Betsy, our milk cow, you'd just about have to pay us to go near one of those animals.

No sooner had daddy slapped one of those cows across the rump, raising a cloud of dust and hair, than a dilapidated Ford pickup truck approached from the opposite direction. A short, pudgy, middle-aged man with a long, scraggly beard stepped out of the truck. "Howdy!" he said to my daddy before he started complaining. "Damn cows!" he cussed at them. "They ain't got no better sense than to get out in the road where they can get run over. Damn heifers are always breaking down a fence and running off. I ought to sell all 'em." He spread his arms wide to include all the cattle currently in the road.

"Watch your language. My wife and young'uns are in the car." Daddy's righteous voice conveyed more than his stern look. He might curse a blue streak himself, but nobody else was allowed to curse around his family.

"Shucks, man, I'm sorry! I didn't mean to be cussing at anybody but these damn cows." He stood with hands on both hips staring at the beasts like he wanted to kill them. Ben and I giggled at his continuing profanity.

"Can I help you get them back home?" daddy offered, checking his watch. I know he had to be thinking that if he helped this cursing character, we'd be late for church.

"Naw, me and my boys will get 'em moving," Mr. Profanity said. Two short, fat teenage boys wearing faded dungarees and dingy undershirts hopped off the back of the truck, armed with cattle prods and halters. They immediately began to herd the wayward cattle back down the road to their over-grazed brown pasture, but not before one of them raised her tail to drop a fresh smelly "meadow muffin" in our path.

Mr. Profanity took off his grimy, gray baseball cap and scratched his head, separating strands of mousy brown hair that looked like it had been lacquered with lard. His beady eyes examined daddy from head to foot like he hadn't seen him until now. "Why, you're wearing your Sunday-go-to-meeting clothes. Are you going to preaching this morning?"

"As a matter of fact, we are going out here to Holy Bible Believers' Church where my first cousin, Charley Hill, is the minister. We need to be on our way." Daddy got back into the car and sped toward the church, pulling into the gravel parking lot at 10:59 a.m.

Holy Bible Believers' Church was a little, white, rectangular building that only looked like a church because it had a small wooden cross attached to the roof. Anyone driving down State Route 57 between Chatham and MacKenzie might miss it if it weren't for the sign that some church member had erected in the front grassy area a few years back. As we parked next to the sign I noticed that the sun had already faded the letters on it. I also noticed that someone had planted some flowers in pots by the bottom step going into the church. They had wilted red, yellow, and pink blooms, but no smell that I could tell. As churches went, this one was smaller and plainer than most of the ones around home.

The good thing about getting to church just as Sunday services were starting was that we didn't have to be in there for very long. This morning's service followed the usual pattern of praying, singing, praying, preaching, passing the collection plate, praying, and singing some more. For most kids, it was a matter of standing, sitting, trying to keep still, squirming, fidgeting, and doodling on the hymnal pages, then standing some more.

This morning I tried to pay attention to hear what Cousin Charley would say that might help me to decide what to do about these secrets I was carrying around—to see what Cousin Charley had to say about sin and sinners. As often happened, something else grabbed my attention. This time it was a cardinal chirping in a maple tree outside a window that caught my eye. I knew by its distinctive crest and feathers that it was a male cardinal because the female has only a smattering of red feathers in her mostly brown coat. We learned all about the cardinals when I was in fourth grade because they are the state bird of Virginia. On a limb a little higher up, I spotted a female near a nest where three almost-grown birds seemed to be fighting for space. I nudged Ben with my elbow and nodded toward the window.

"Probably her second family this year," I whispered. I wondered how many eggs she had laid, recalling that a female cardinal can lay about ten eggs a year, but most of the time they don't all hatch. Cardinals became my favorite birds because they don't migrate in autumn like many other species do. In the wintertime, cardinals perching on the branches of a snow-sprinkled white pine look like they belong on a Christmas card. I wondered how old these two birds might be, since some of them can live up to fifteen years. Thinking about these birds was a pleasant diversion, but the cardinals flew away, taking with them a yearning that I had—to be as free as they were: free of secrets, free of bad dreams, free of the pressure I was feeling about getting baptized. There was little to do now but turn my attention back to the Sunday morning service.

Tuning in to Cousin Charley's sermon, I heard words about the wrath of God inflicting vengeance when his commandments were not obeyed. People suffered hunger and famine, plagues and dreadful diseases, beheadings and other mutilations because they did not walk in the way of the Lord. Mercy, I thought. Fear of punishment from my parents had kept me on a pretty narrow path for almost twelve years. Now I was hearing that fear of God's punishment should guide me all the days of my life.

Fear of going to hell loomed so large in my mind that it weighed me down like a hat made of marble might do. Did fear of God's punishment mean I could never have any fun? What happened to God loving us for doing what's right—for believing in him and obeying his commandments? These were just a few more questions to ponder before I made my decision about getting "saved."

I noticed that daddy was paying close attention to what Cousin Charley had to say today.

Cousin Charley, daddy's first cousin and lifelong best friend, often invited us to attend Sunday services at Holy Bible Believers' Church. Daddy was no Bible believer, but sometimes he preferred to go to Cousin Charley's church rather than to Healing Waters Gospel Church, where mama was a member. Mama said that was because daddy thought Cousin Charley's word was the gospel, whether it had anything to do with the Bible or not.

Perhaps daddy liked Holy Bible Believers' Church better because he liked Cousin Charley so much. Maybe he liked it because most of the people there were poor tobacco farmers like him. When the collection plate was passed in the summer months, everybody knew that the contributions would be small. Daddy always said it was a good thing that Cousin Charley owned an insurance agency and sold the other kind of "life" insurance. Cousin Charley liked to say he had his people covered—coming and going.

The Believers followed a simple creed—live according to the teachings of the Holy Bible. They took the word of God quite literally, especially the part about how a woman ought to obey a man. The men in this church dictated that women should not cut their hair and should wear only dresses that covered most of their body, even when they were working in tobacco. Women should wear neither makeup nor jewelry and should allow the men in their families to make all of the decisions and usually to mete out any punishments that they saw fit. The folks at Healing Waters Gospel Church used the same King James Version of the Bible, but they didn't have any restrictions on what people wore. Yet they did have a lot to say about what a person did, like not drinking, dancing, and fornicating.

Only members of the Holy Bible Believers' Church were allowed to take communion, which was offered only on a few holy days each year. At Healing Waters Gospel Church, communion was served every Sunday morning to anyone who was a baptized Christian. Since daddy, Ben, and I had not been baptized, we never took communion anywhere, except for one time when I grabbed a handful of those little crackers when they were passed around, along with a thimble-size glass of grape juice. Mama slapped me right there in church for taking something she said I had no right to have. I told her I was hungry and that I just wanted a little snack. Why would the church not want me to eat when I was hungry? Sometimes I wondered if either church was the right one for me.

Amidst my thoughts about the differences between the Bible Believers and the Gospel crowd, a commotion in the pew in front of me caught my eye. Not wanting Ben to miss out on anything, I tapped him on the shoulder and pointed in that direction. The little Loveless boys were about to get into some serious trouble.

Sister Sarah Loveless, who was no kin of ours, had two little boys who were known for being rowdy in church: Billy, age six, and Bobby, age eight. "Little Hell Raisers" is what mama called them. She had said many times that no child of hers would ever act like them and get by with it. "I'd take a switch to them. I'd beat their little bottoms until they couldn't sit down!" she said.

This Sunday morning, those two were kicking the pew in front of them, punching each other, squirming around, talking out loud, and just being obnoxious. Their grandma tried her best to get them to sit still and be quiet until the service was over. Nothing she did made any difference.

Their mama was singing in the choir while their daddy, Brother Samuel, was leading the choir. He had his back to the action, but their mama could see everything from her elevated position. Sister Sarah must have seen and heard just about all she could tolerate when suddenly a radio came on somewhere in the congregation.

"Good morning, out there in radio land. This is Wes Walker coming to you from WBTM. That's World's Best Tobacco Market, or World's Biggest Textile Mill. Take your pick. They're both right here in Danville, Virginia."

Before the boys' grandma could shut the transistor radio off, Sister Sarah had stomped out of the choir loft, right past Cousin Charley and down the aisle. She was madder than an old wet hen. Her big bosoms bounced up and down as she took lengthy strides, sending shock waves across the creaky, old wooden boards of the church. Ben elbowed me and then moved his hands up and down to mimic the action of her boobs. I sat there with my hand over my mouth to keep from giggling.

Sister Sarah grabbed the older boy by the ear and yanked him out of the pew, where she proceeded to give him a whipping he wouldn't soon forget. Her big right hand hit his behind *ka-whop, ka-whop, ka-whop*, again and again. The whole congregation sat staring, wide-eyed, astonished at what was happening. They were probably thinking what I was thinking—their daddy is the one who is supposed to be whipping him!

While she was whipping Bobby, little Billy got down on the floor and scampered around. I was sitting close enough to see that he was trying to capture a frog that had wiggled out of his pocket. Billy would try to grab it. The frog would hop first one way, then another. He was zigzagging his way to the back door with Billy in close pursuit. No sooner had he caught that frog than Sister Sarah, having finished with Bobby, caught up with Billy. She shoved him out the door long enough to get rid of the frog, then brought him back inside to whip him in front of God and everybody.

I stole a glance at Cousin Charley, who had stopped preaching in mid-sentence, mouth open. He just stood there, his long face frozen, his piercing brown eyes staring at the commotion until Sister Sarah, with her head held high, her chin jutting out, her eyes fixed on the altar, walked briskly back to the choir loft. Some folks nodded approval as she strode by.

"Spare the rod and spoil the child," Cousin Charley said, appearing to read from the Bible, then went right back to his sermon like nothing had happened. I wondered, does his apparent approval mean whipping a kid is not wrong in the eyes of God, so long as you don't kill him?

What about parents who do things that are wrong? Like mama and that man. I know that was wrong, but was it wrong of me to keep it a secret? Was I sinning by not telling daddy what I had seen? The Sunday morning service ended with no time for me to think about anything more.

On this particularly eventful day, we drove straight from church to Cousin Charley's home, a small yellow stucco house on a quiet street in Martinsville. As soon as his wife, Eva, opened the back door for us, we were greeted with the aroma of fried chicken. I couldn't wait to eat some of those drumsticks.

I always loved eating at their house because Eva was an excellent cook who seemed to know just what we liked. On this day, she had baked ham, green beans with new potatoes boiled on top, corn on the cob, green peas, coleslaw, butter beans, deviled eggs, macaroni and cheese, sliced ripe tomatoes, pickled beets, corn bread, biscuits, and lots of sweet tea, in addition to the fried chicken. Our devil's food cake and peach cobbler would make a fine finish to this late summer feast.

This meal was nothing fancy, just plain, good food, especially the biscuits. They came out of these little cans that Cousin Eva opened by smacking them against the edge of the yellow kitchen counter. *Ka-whap pop, ka-whap pop!* I thought they were the best-tasting biscuits that I'd ever had, since they were store bought and not at all like the ones mama made from flour, buttermilk, and lard at home.

Just thinking about Eva's meals made me hungrier. So did thinking about the devil's food cake with seven minute frosting that mama had made for our dinner. She always made it for special occasions and whenever kinfolk came to our house to eat. Mama could put out a fine spread too, which she did every day for us. As I surveyed this day's colorful dishes and inhaled the mouthwatering scents of all this food, I knew that consuming so much of it—gluttony—was a sin. However, my thoughts on the wickedness of worshiping food vanished the second Eva announced that dinner was ready.

Squeezing around the light green Formica and chrome kitchen table, eager to consume all that good food, we took our seats, knowing that we couldn't eat a bite before grace was said over this meal. Ben immediately volunteered. I was shocked because my older brother never prayed out loud. At least, as far as I knew, he never had until now. I wondered what he would say.

Eva smiled at him, patted his shoulder and said, "Son, you go right ahead now and say grace. The good Lord will be happy to hear from you."

Cousin Charley was beaming, probably thinking he had found a convert. Mama and daddy exchanged a look of surprise and concern. I started to snicker but caught myself before mama could stop me with one of her looks that said, "Do that and you're dead!"

"God is great," Ben began. "God is good. And we thank Him for this food."

Then there was this long silence. It seemed to me that we sat there with our heads bowed and eyes closed for almost five minutes without anybody saying anything. The food was getting cold. My stomach was growling. I wanted him to hurry up. I wondered if Ben had fallen asleep, so I kicked him under the table.

"Ouch! Oh God, I forgot the rest!" he cried while kicking me back, a swift move that glanced off the side of my skinny little legs.

"Amen," daddy came to his rescue while the rest of us giggled, even Cousin Charley.

"That's all right, son," Eva said, patting Ben on his shoulder again. "Here, you take the first piece of chicken and pass it around."

Ben's face reflected all the embarrassment that I knew he must have felt, but his chagrin at forgetting the words to this familiar little prayer was quickly dispelled by his voracious appetite. "Chagrin…" "dispelled…" "voracious…" my little brain was working overtime that day as I recalled more of the vocabulary words Mrs. Rivers had taught us the year before. I knew my beloved teacher would be proud of me.

I stared at Ben a moment more. Short and small for a boy soon to be a teenager, Ben could still put away some food. His usually kind aqua eyes shot darts at me as he took a chicken drumstick and passed the platter to mama. Bowls went back and forth and across the table amid exclamations about how good everything looked and smelled.

I sat there feeling very smug, knowing I could have finished the prayer for Ben but didn't. Then my conscience kicked in. Was this failure to help him wrong? I knew that kicking him under the table was mean. Was my being smug about it what was truly wrong? I was having a lot of trouble figuring out what was right and wrong in my world and whether any of the "wrongs" were considered sins in the eyes of God. I got lost in my own conscience, even as I chewed the meat right off the drumstick. Finally, I concluded that this little episode couldn't count for much with God—otherwise, I would be sinning all the time.

We sat at the table, eating and talking for a long time. Mostly it was the adults doing the talking while Ben and I listened. Bug had been fed and was now fast asleep in the Hills' extra bedroom. Mama and daddy had raised us to be seen and not heard, so quietly pursuing our own thoughts while occasionally tuning in to their conversations was easy for us.

Mama asked Cousin Charley, "Have you ever had anything happen during church like what happened this morning?"

"Never," he replied, as he shook his head. "I didn't know what was going on."

"Those young'uns got what was coming to 'em, by Jings," daddy stated, his steel gray eyes flashing anger ("By Jings" was as close as daddy usually came to cussing while he was around Cousin Charley).

"Yeah, those boys got what they needed, all right. There I was in the middle of my sermon when that radio came on. Then Sister Sarah bolted from the choir loft and whipped past me like a mama on a mission!" Cousin Charley chuckled, his brown eyes dancing with merriment.

"I don't 'spect they'll be a problem from now on," Eva giggled, "will they, Bunny?"

My ears perked up when I heard Eva call Cousin Charley "Bunny." She always called him that, unless she was at church. I wanted to ask her why. He had big ears, but not floppy ones, and his brown crew cut, all lathered up with Brylcream, didn't look like rabbit fur to me. When I asked mama and daddy once about this strange nick-name, daddy said it was because Cousin Charley had some habits like a rabbit. He had winked at mama and the two of them had laughed, like it was some sort of private joke. I thought maybe Cousin Charley just wiggled his big ole beak of a nose when he ate carrots. Just to be sure, I would ask Eva sometime when nobody else was around.

Mama and daddy didn't like for me to ask personal questions. It seemed to me that mama thought asking a question that began with "Why" was rude, thoughtless, and annoying; but in school, Mrs. Rivers told us to always ask questions because it helped us to learn more. I sure hated to limit myself to listening and drawing my own conclusions based on *my* limited knowledge of the world. There was so much I wanted to learn—about God, about life, about everything.

There was a lull in the conversation while we all chewed our food. Now was my chance to ask a question that had been troubling me, so I spoke up. "Cousin Charley, how old do you think a person needs to be to join a church?"

Mama immediately glared at me, while Ben and daddy looked back and forth between mama and me. Cousin Charley must have noticed that my question had brought some tension to the table. He cleared his throat a couple of times and then said, "Well, Darla Mae, you are never too old or too young to give your life to the Lord. Some churches baptize babies with the understanding that their parents will raise them according to the beliefs and practices of that church. Some old folks are on their deathbed before they ask God to forgive their sins. While most churches will gladly accept anyone at any age, some of us think a child needs to be around twelve years old before she makes a profession of faith."

Cousin Charley glanced at daddy, then mama, then back at me before he continued, "You see, Christ left his parents to go out into the world when he was twelve, so that age has some significance to those of us who believe in him. I don't know if a child younger than that would actually understand what he was doing. Why did you ask? Are you thinking about joining my church?"

Mama said, "No, she's not," before I could get a word out of my mouth. This time I glared at her.

"What Alene is saying is that we think Darla Mae is too young to join a church, regardless of which one it is," daddy said, in an obvious attempt to keep peace and harmony among us.

"Besides, she's scared to death of drowning," Ben added, holding his nose and pretending to holler for help. We couldn't help but laugh.

Cousin Charley chuckled. "I've only dropped one lady when I baptized her. She swam away and never came back to church." He looked at Eva and both of them laughed loudly.

"Bunny, don't be telling such tales. I not only came back to church, I married you!"

"She'd already been baptized when she was a teenager, but decided to rededicate her life to God. She asked me to baptize her again, and well, she just slipped up in that muddy creek." Cousin Charley's eyes seemed to dance with delight as he shared more of the details. By this time we were all laughing again. I wasn't about to ask another question that might change the good feelings that we had among us just then.

Chapter 8

The talking went on, back and forth, for a really long time, which was fine by me. I enjoyed listening to adult conversation, or pretending to listen while allowing my mind to take detours through its young, fertile fields as I tried to make sense of life's mysteries. Some things in my world seemed wrong to me, but were considered right by almost everyone else. What happened to a person after she died troubled me. What did it really mean to be "saved," and how in the world could anyone pray without ceasing? I wondered if what I saw mama doing with that man was considered right by her. Often times, I'd get so involved with my own thoughts that someone would have to call my name to get me back to what was happening at the moment.

"Darla Mae! Darla Mae! Are you all right?" mama asked, somewhat urgently.

"Huh?" I asked. "I mean, ma'am," I remembered just in time.

"Go get your little brother and bring him in here."

"Yes, ma'am," I replied as I pried my bare legs off the sticky, hot, vinyl seat, making squeaky sucking noises, the kind people make when they "break wind." That embarrassed me and made Ben snicker.

Going down the narrow hallway, I heard mama's instruction, "If he's wet, change him first." I was glad my back was to her so she couldn't see I was making a face as I considered the excellent possibility that he would be more than wet. Changing baby diapers was my most disgusting chore, worse than mucking the cow's stall.

Bug was crying now, the way he usually did upon awakening. I hurried to pick him up before he could roll off the bed. He was lying on his back, beating his little fists in the air and kicking his feet hard against the mattress. His small, oval face was all screwed up and red from crying. There was no doubt about the state of his diaper.

I carried him to the bathroom, where I placed him on a fluffy, green rug in front of the tub to change him. He'd stopped crying now and was sweetly cooing, his big brown eyes examining the pink walls and multi-colored fish that hung over the commode. At six months old, he was quite alert and curious about his surroundings.

"I'm going to get you cleaned up," I told him.

He laughed at the sound of my voice, the way that he often did when I read to him. Regardless of what I read, whether story books, *The Progressive Farmer*, or the back of a cereal box, Bug seemed to find it amusing. Just the other day I'd been reading the obituaries out of our weekly newspaper, *The Star Tribune*, when he shrieked with laughter. (Some of those old names, like Loudellia Dumfries and Seymour Tinkles *were* funny.) Bug reached for my face, tried to put a finger in my mouth, and stared into the opening as if he wanted to see what made the sound.

"Phew whew!" I said, turning my nose away from him. Bug giggled again, apparently delighted that he could produce a reaction from me.

I held my breath, trying not to inhale the pungent stench and trying not to gag as I removed the dirty diaper. At that very moment I made one of the many decisions I often found myself making about my future. I promised myself never to have a baby if this is what I would have to do. Using bathroom tissue, I wiped him clean. Then I washed and powdered his little bottom before putting on the clean diaper.

Soon after Bug was born, mama had taught me how to fold the cloth diaper, how to place it under him, bring it up just so, then pin it on each side with big plastic-coated diaper pins, being careful not to stick the sharp end into him. Getting that diaper tight enough to stay on without sticking a pin in the baby took some practice. I thought there had to be a better way, so one day I got a roll of daddy's duct tape and taped the diaper together. Mama about had a hissy fit! I giggled to myself remembering her reaction.

I was still giggling when I propped Bug up against the side of the tub while I rinsed out the dirty diaper in the commode. More yucky work. Then I washed it out in the sink before storing it in a plastic bag that we brought along for that purpose. I surely didn't want to do this again today. If that kid hadn't been such a little bundle of joy, I probably wouldn't have been able to change a diaper at all.

Finally finished with the unpleasantness, I swung Bug up to my hip and walked him around the tiny room, naming the objects. We felt the smooth, white porcelain sink, the cool, hard surface of the tub, the slick vinyl of the shower curtain, the fuzzy softness of the commode cover, and the rough, uneven shape of the multicolored ceramic fish hanging over it. Bug's giggles and shrieks, as I rubbed his hand over each one, told me I was doing a good job of entertaining him.

I stopped in front of the mirror, where Bug could see his reflection and I could examine my own. Skinny, I thought as I looked at myself. My face, my arms, my body, my legs, even my feet were pencil-thin. I tried smiling at myself, which made my green eyes twinkle and my tanned cheeks go rosy. Now if I didn't have crooked buckteeth, I'd look better, I thought to myself, but I knew I would never be a Miss America.

Being too interested in one's appearance was a sin in the eyes of the Bible Believers. "Vanity," they called it. Not wanting to be vain is why their womenfolk didn't wear makeup, although many of them could use some fixing up. They wore plain clothes and no jewelry, except for wedding rings. As if that wasn't enough, they let their hair grow to incredible lengths and wrapped it up in buns. You'd think they had the power of Samson in those long locks, especially ole butt-beating Sister Sarah. I tried to imagine myself looking like her or one of the other women there in about twenty years. Not a pretty picture, I thought.

Bug reached for the mirror, trying to touch the boy who was looking back at him. His luminous brown eyes grew wider as I held him closer to it. Mine grew wider too, as I realized that Bug didn't look like anybody else in our family. His black hair and dark skin were in sharp contrast to the rest of us. Which distant relative did he look like? How come one kid got all the good looks? I wondered.

I decided that I would ask mama that question someday, but I already knew her answer. "That's for me to know and you to wonder about." So, I could be wondering for months, wondering if I would ever know the answers to all the questions that I had about adult stuff. Wondering if sin was somehow involved.

Chapter 9

"*D*arla Mae, come on out of there. Somebody else might need to use the bathroom," I heard mama call from outside the door. I opened the door, handed the baby to her, and turned to retrieve the plastic bag containing the soiled diaper.

"Take that out to the car," mama said as she checked the diaper to be sure that I had pinned it tight enough.

"OK." I slipped past her on my way to the back door. Thankfully, daddy had parked the Dream Wagon in the shade and left the windows rolled down. After I put the bag on the floor of the back seat, I hurried back inside the house where Eva was busy clearing the table.

"I can help with the dishes." If I stayed in the kitchen I could listen to, and maybe even participate in, the adult conversation.

"Why, that's mighty sweet of you to offer, Darla Mae." Eva smiled at me as she set dirty plates on the counter next to the sink. "Would you rather wash or dry?"

"I do both at home," I told her.

"Well, you wash. Your mama can dry. And I'll put them away, since I know where everything goes," she concluded while rummaging through a drawer containing dishtowels, aprons, and such.

"Let me tie this little apron around you. I wouldn't want you to get that pretty new dress dirty," Eva added as she tied a yellow, ruffled apron around my waist and flipped the bib over my head. It was so big it covered almost all of me.

I filled the sink with hot water, so hot it almost burned my hands. That was what I was used to doing—washing dishes in extremely hot water to be sure they were free of germs. At home I would pour boiling water from the teakettle over them to rinse them, too, scalding them to be sure it was safe to eat off them.

There were lots of dishes to be washed. I scraped and stacked them, putting the same size pieces together, before I started washing the glasses. I also wiped crumbs and spills off a spot on the counter where mama could put the dishes after she dried them.

"You are just so organized," Eva said, noticing how I had arranged everything.

"She does right well. She's got big enough to be a lot of help to me," mama said. She rinsed a glass, carefully dried it, and then held it up to the light to be sure that it didn't have lipstick smudges or anything still on it.

"You'll have to let her come up here and stay with me a while. I'd like to have some help around the house," Eva said, giving me a hug around the shoulders.

"You'll just have to have your own little girl," mama replied.

"Alene, you know I would have had a house full of children if I could," Eva answered as she covered a platter of leftover ham and stored it in the refrigerator.

Mama raised an eyebrow in her direction before Eva reconsidered. "Well, one or two anyway. You know, being the oldest child, I had to help raise all my brothers and sisters. There were nine of us, so when Charley and I got married, I wasn't eager to see any more babies right away."

Drying another glass, one with flowers painted in a border around its middle that looked just like the ones we got out of Duz detergent boxes, mama found a fleck of something on it and passed it back to me to rewash. She always inspected whatever I did to make sure that I was doing it just right. Cleanliness was next to Godliness in mama's mind.

I glanced at Eva as I picked up some plates to wash. Her pleasant, square face suddenly looked sad. Her blue eyes were moist, like she was about to cry.

"It don't seem right that some people who have so much to offer don't have children and some of us who have so little have more children than we want," mama said, her hand stopped for a moment over the center of the plate she was drying.

Mama's words, "more children than we want," raced through my brain like a bolt of lightning, igniting a memory I had tried to bury. I kept washing dishes, glad for something to do that kept my hands busy and my eyes off mama.

My thoughts rushed back to a conversation that I had overheard in August of the year before. We were visiting friends of my parents, whose house had a rope swing hanging from a sturdy branch of an old oak tree. Being on a swing always gave me a feeling of freedom and exhilaration, a feeling I thought would be with me for a lifetime. I'd bend my legs and lean forward, pumping, going higher and higher. That swing seemed to call to me, a call stronger than anything that I'd ever known. I was a jumble of emotions that day, feeling out of sorts with myself, lost somewhere between childhood and adolescence. Maybe spending some time in that swing could help me figure out where I was.

I went outside, pushed the seat away from me, and jumped on the narrow, wooden board as it swung back toward me. Up and away I went, again and again, enjoying the scent of flowers in bloom as I rushed past them until their colors became a dizzying blur. In those moments, the joyous, carefree present was the only place I wanted to be.

I'd been swinging for a good, long while when I heard the front door open. Mama and her friend, Lois, had come outside to look at some flowers. I had hopped off the swing and hid behind a bush nearby when I heard them coming, thinking I would make a game of not being discovered. Besides, I liked eavesdropping on adult conversations.

"Looks like I am going to have another baby," mama said to Lois.

"What?" Lois' perfectly round face registered how shocked she was. She pushed a stray brown hair away from her left eye. "Aren't you getting a little old for that?" Lois asked just the question I wanted to ask.

"Just because you're a little old for babies don't mean that you're too old for s-e-x," mama said as she broke a bloom off a blue hydrangea.

"Well, I declare!" Lois' brown eyes became huge and seemed to pop right out of her head.

I knew I should stop listening at this point, but I just couldn't make myself put my hands over my ears. A baby! My mama was going to have a baby. I was going to have a little brother or sister. I immediately hoped it would be a girl, a darling little girl that I could dress up and pretend she was my doll baby. Then I remembered last Christmas, when mama told me that I was too old to be playing with dolls, too old for such kid stuff.

"And I'll tell you something else, but don't you breathe it to anybody," mama continued, waving the hydrangea bloom so hard that it was dropping some of its petals.

"Oh no, I won't tell a soul," Lois promised as she stood there staring at my mama like she was somebody from outer space.

"Well, I'd been planning to leave Walt," mama confided, her eyes downcast.

"Leave Walt?" Lois asked, her voice trembling in disbelief.

I couldn't believe my ears either. My mama wanted to leave my daddy. I wanted to scream, "No! No! You can't do that!" But I was afraid that they'd hear me and know that I'd been eavesdropping. Still, why on earth mama would want to leave daddy? She seemed to love him. Or did she? But why wouldn't she? He didn't drink, gamble, or run around with other women. He didn't even smoke cigarettes anymore. Daddy didn't drive fast cars. He didn't spend much money. Of course there wasn't much money to spend. Their little tobacco crop didn't produce much income. The extra work that daddy did occasionally, baling hay and plowing fields for other people, didn't earn much money either.

Maybe money was the problem. Maybe mama wanted to work a public job so she could build a new house or buy some new clothes so she didn't have to make everything from feed sacks and mill cloth. Money had to be the reason mama would leave.

Suddenly the image that I had tried hard to put out of my mind returned. Mama in bed with that man. Maybe he was the real reason she wanted to leave.

I wondered what all this would mean for Ben and me. Where would we live? Would we stay with her or with daddy? Would we ever see daddy again if we didn't live with him? What if Ben stayed with him and I went with mama? This news was so depressing. I started to cry.

I stood there behind that evergreen bush, my shoulders slumped, my heart sinking right into the ground. Mama's voice brought me back from my wondering. She and Lois were now standing opposite the bush where I was hiding. Whatever had been said while I was hanging out with my own thoughts, I'll never know.

"Now I won't be able to leave. Never. By the time this baby is grown, I'll be too old to get out on my own." Mama seemed resigned to her fate, but not the least bit happy about it.

So, she wasn't going to leave daddy after all. But she also didn't want this baby. I was relieved and sad at the same time. Now I wanted them to hurry on back into the house so I could come out of my hiding place and swing some more. I needed the time alone, up there among the tree limbs, to figure out how I could ever live with another terrible secret.

Chapter 10

"Darla Mae, where is your mind? Girl, you need to pay attention to what you're doing. There's a spot on this plate and this one, too." Mama's irritation was evident as she handed the soiled plates back to me. There was no way I was going to tell her where my mind had been. I had decided on that day long ago, while still hiding behind that bush, that some family secrets are best kept buried. As far as I was concerned, that was where mama's secrets were going to stay. Unless I *had* to tell them.

"I'm sorry, mama," I said as I scratched the spots from the dirty plates with a fingernail, washed and rinsed them again, happy to prove myself competent for this task. Happy, too, that Eva trusted me to handle her pretty dishes, which she had obviously bought at a store (we got most of ours as prizes packed inside twenty-five–pound bags of flour). I would try to be extra careful with Eva's dishes, and not take any chances of breaking them.

If I'd broken anything, daddy would have insisted on paying for it, which meant that he'd be really mad at me. Daddy probably wouldn't whip me if he could think of another way to punish me. More than likely he'd make me pick horn worms off those nasty old tobacco plants for nothing to work off my debt.

The day before he'd given Ben and me a nickel for each hornworm that we collected in our empty one gallon Karo syrup buckets. Picking hornworms off tobacco plants is a disgusting task, especially on a sticky hot day, but being in the field with my older brother made the ordeal bearable, even fun at times. Ben and I teased each other, chased each other down the rows of tobacco, threatened each other with clods of dirt tossed at our bare feet, and stopped to eat sweet, red, ripe tomatoes from vines that daddy purposely planted in the tobacco rows. "Sometimes you just need a snack when you're working out here," he'd explained to mama about the tomatoes and a few watermelon vines that were scattered in the field among the tobacco plants.

Those tomatoes were about as ugly as any tomatoes I've ever seen. Most of them were all curled up around the stem with grooves radiating out from the center. Occasionally there would be one with just two grooves and an extra little growth of tomato hanging down between them. I got a kick out of biting off that little growth before attacking the rest of the tomato, sending its juices and seeds flying, usually all over me and anything else that was close by.

Ben and I picked several of the ripest tomatoes and ran down to the end of the row where we sat to eat them in the shade of an old oak tree. Many similar trees grew on our farm, the ones with enormous roots that run for a couple of yards above ground before disappearing into the dark earth. These roots made fine seats for tired workers like Ben and me. He plopped on the biggest root while I piled my tomatoes on the ground next to a root nearby.

We'd left a half-gallon Mason jar filled with cold water under the tree that morning. I removed the lid, took a long swig of that cool, refreshing water and passed it over to Ben, who used some of it to wash a tomato before taking a drink. Both of us were grateful that mama had put some ice cubes in it, even though most had melted on the way to the tobacco field.

I scooped up a fistful of sand, poured a little water into it and rubbed it over my hands and bare arms to remove the tobacco gum that had accumulated on them. Black and sticky, this tar-like substance from the tobacco leaves clung to anything that touched it and stubbornly refused to be washed off unless you had some kind of scouring powder. Sand worked OK, at least well enough for me to eat some of those tempting tomatoes. Ben just ate his tomatoes with his dirty hands, something I could never do. Boys like Ben seem to know nothing about dirt and germs.

I washed my tomatoes, then settled between two roots and leaned back on the tree trunk to savor them. As soon as I had taken a bite, a deafening noise exploded around us, causing both of us to spit tomato in all directions as we jumped up to see what was happening.

"Look! Up there!" Ben shouted as he pointed to the clear blue sky where a dark, familiar shape was streaking high overhead.

"That was a sonic boom! That jet just broke the sound barrier!" he explained in a voice that conveyed more excitement than I think I'd ever seen in my usually easygoing brother. His sharp eyes followed the jet until it was completely out of sight.

"I'm going to fly one of those someday." Ben's voice sounded confident, determined. "I'm going to fly away from here and never come back."

"How do you think you're going to do that?" I looked him square in the eye, challenging him to give me a straight answer. Ben had been known to lead me astray, taking advantage of my being younger and less knowledgeable by telling me all sorts of stuff just to see how gullible I was.

"I'll do what Jerry Adams did. I'll join the Navy and let their pilots teach me to fly. Then I'll travel all over the world." Ben's face took on a dreamy quality as he returned his gaze toward the distant sky where the jet had already disappeared from sight.

Jerry Adams was a local boy who'd dropped out of high school, lied about his age, and joined the Navy. Some folks said he'd gone into the military to avoid a shotgun wedding at home. Others laughed that he now had a drill sergeant giving him his marching orders instead of that pretty little wife he could have had. I really didn't know why people took shotguns to weddings, but I didn't blame Jerry for not getting married while he was still so young—sixteen, I think.

Jerry told my daddy that he had only dated that girl a couple of times and had quit asking her out because she came on too strong. I asked daddy what that meant and he told me to go ask my mama. Of course, mama told me that was for her to know and me to wonder about. So all I knew was that she was a lot younger than Jerry. She was short with chin-length jet-black hair, ice-blue eyes, big boobs that looked bumpy like they'd been stuffed with toilet tissue, and a skinny butt that swung from side to side when she walked. Most people at school referred to her as "Prissy" and laughed about how they'd put a swing like hers on their back porch. Miss Prissy was always kissing and hanging on to some boy on our school bus. One day I overheard her bragging about how she sometimes sneaked off from school, smoked, drank, and got wild, then lied to her mama about being sick when she really wasn't sick at all. Jerry Adams hardly ever talked to her. He was just too smart for that girl.

When Jerry came home wearing his Navy uniform with that crazy sailor collar and bell-bottomed pants, I thought he looked like a Greek god. Not that I had any idea what a Greek god looked like, since there weren't any pictures in that mythology book Mrs. Rivers had given me to read, but at six feet tall with a slender body, golden blonde hair and eyes as dark blue as the autumn sky, I thought he was perfect. You could see his face reflected in his spit-shined shoes.

The fact that he talked with me about school, music, and such always made me feel special, even though he was about eight years older than me. Jerry came from a big family with lots of younger brothers and sisters, which might explain why he was so kind to Ben and me. Just thinking about him made me smile. If Ben was going to go off to the Navy and fly planes with Jerry Adams, I wanted to go too.

"Oh, take me with you. You know I'd do almost anything to get away from these tobacco fields."

"Sis, you have a long way to go before you finish school." Ben's aqua eyes teased me. "Besides, the Navy probably wouldn't take a sawed-off, bow-legged, knot-kneed runt like you!"

I hurled a hard clod, about the size of a brick, at his feet. That solid chunk of Virginia clay shattered and sent a spray of red dirt over his feet and legs. Ben grabbed a small rock and aimed it at my big toe, just barely missing it and Kati, who had trotted over to the tobacco field with us.

"Someday I'm going to be pretty. When I get enough money to do it, I'll have my teeth straightened and buy a wig to cover up this mousey, limp hair. My legs will grow, too. All I have to do is get older, then I won't be so short. I'll join the Navy and work really hard until I outrank you!" I vowed, biting into my third tomato.

Ben turned away from me and snickered. "No, you won't! You'll just marry an old farm boy and raise yourself a house full of young'uns. Maybe get a job at Dan River Mills or one of the garment factories. And you'll get uglier and fatter every year."

"I will not!" I shouted at him.

"Will, too," Ben continued to harass me while a smirk played over his dirty, tanned face.

There was nothing handy to throw at him, so I decided to ignore him while I finished my tomatoes. Those ugly ole tomatoes tasted so good, their flavor a slice of heaven that woke up all the right taste buds. They made my mouth happy. I could have eaten a dozen all by myself, but daddy had come to the field to check on us, so Ben and I had to get back to our tasks.

We worked in silence for a while, searching the tobacco leaves for telltale signs of the presence of hornworms. Those little multi-legged critters could devour a tobacco plant a day, partially destroying leaves, making them good for nothing but the trash pile. Removing them meant the tobacco would weigh more and be worth more.

Our family needed our tobacco to be of the best quality and to weigh as much as possible so that we could get all the money we could out of it. This mindless work gave me time to consider all sorts of situations and outcomes.

"Ben, do you think Jerry could go to hell for lying about his age to get in the Navy?" I asked after mulling this possibility over in my mind as I searched the plants for more hornworms.

"What?" Ben stopped and stared at me, still holding on to a wiggling green worm by its horns.

I repeated the question, all the time keeping my eyes on that worm he was holding in case he decided to throw it on me. Those little critters stink to high heavens if they get squashed. No way did I want one of them squashed on me. "One of the Ten Commandments is that we should not bear false witness… not tell a lie. Since Jerry lied to get in the Navy, do you think he will go to hell?"

"Hell no! Why don't you stop being so stupid? If anybody goes to hell, it's going to be you for being such a *%#&*# pest. You are worrying about religion and dying and hell all the time. What's got into you?" Ben glared at me, his eyes suddenly intensely dark. "Why can't you just relax and enjoy life, like me?" He smiled as he extended his left arm toward me and dangled the worm in my face.

I backed away from the disgusting green larva and from Ben's words that left me feeling painfully frustrated. If he had been willing to discuss the lying issue with me, I was going to tell him about the bad dreams I'd been having. I really wanted to talk with someone about these dreams, someone who wouldn't think I needed to be shipped off to that insane hospital in Staunton. If he had listened, I would have told him about mama, too. Now that I knew Ben thought I was being stupid for wondering about the afterlife, all I could think to do was to threaten him with, "I'm going tell mama that you cussed."

Ben tossed the hornworm into his bucket and moved over to the next tobacco plant. I searched the plant in front of me, before quickly moving on to the next and the next. Sweat was rolling off my neck and meandering down my chest before it got absorbed into my cotton panties. I desperately wanted to get out of this blazing hot tobacco field, which I was sure bore a striking resemblance to some place in hell.

Chapter 11

A flash from a camera nearby snapped me out of my reverie. Eva was taking a picture of me there at the sink, washing dishes in that big, yellow, ruffled apron. "You just look so cute. I had to take your picture," she grinned, her light blue eyes twinkling. I gave her a big cheesy smile, one that stretched as wide as my mouth would go, before she took another one of me.

"And I want to get one of all of your family today while everybody is dressed up," Eva said to mama as she dried the last of the pots and pans. I wiped off the table, rinsed out the dishcloth, and hung it up to dry on a little rack that was attached to the wall next to the sink. The three of us went into the living room where Cousin Charley, daddy, and Ben were talking about the newest models of cars on the market.

"Can't beat a Chevrolet," daddy said. "They take you where you want to go and get you back home again. Hardly ever break down. Reliable. That's what I want in a car."

"You can't beat that '57 Chevy Bel Air for style either," Cousin Charley said. "That is one beautiful car. It'll be classic someday."

"I've heard some of the boys at school talking about how fast they can run, too. Over a hundred miles an hour, some of them say. Of course, one of them has a modified Chevy with four in the floor and a 283 Super Turbo-Fire V8 fuel-injected engine under the hood. I've heard that the boys from Museville drag race over there near Chatham about every Saturday night." Ben's face glowed with his knowledge of the local scuttlebutt.

"Better not ever hear of you drag racing or even riding with someone who's racing." Daddy gave Ben a stern look that quickly stifled Ben's enthusiasm.

"Daddy, did you ever drag race?" I had to ask the question, wondering if drag racing was as exciting as Ben made it sound. There was something about a forbidden activity that made it really appealing to me.

Daddy turned his glaring gray eyes on me before saying, "Yeah, I did. Once. And I am lucky that I lived to tell about it. That's how I lost three front teeth." Daddy pointed to the gap in his lower teeth. "They got knocked out when I wrecked the car. My broken ribs healed but these gaps in my front teeth are there forever to remind me not to be so stupid." All of us had heard daddy say he had lost his teeth in an accident, but he'd never told us how the accident happened.

There were questions I wanted to ask him, like where he did his drag racing, how old he was, and what happened when he wrecked, but when I turned my inquisitive eyes to him, I decided to keep quiet. His eyes had started to mist and mine probably did too. I now knew that my daddy had once been young and reckless. Immediately, I wondered if mama had regretted anything that she had done. If she knew that I knew about her and that man, I know she'd have some regrets!

I guess everybody felt a little uncomfortable with daddy's confession. Cousin Charley faked a cough and suggested that we drive out to visit his mother, my Great-Aunt Alice.

"Not before I take a couple of pictures of everybody." Eva held up the camera for all to see that she was ready to play photographer.

She pointed to a modern-style chair, upholstered in beige textured fabric that sat near the front door. "Alene, why don't you sit in that chair and hold Bug? Walt, you stand behind it and a little to the side. Ben, sit on the arm, and Darla Mae, you stand there next to your daddy." Cousin Charley closed the beige pinch-pleated drapes blocking out the bright light that was streaming through the big picture window near us.

We took our places and on the count of three, all of us said "Cheese," except for daddy, who hated having his picture taken and always kept his lips pressed together in a thin smile. Eva took two more shots, moving us around into different arrangements.

"Want me to take one of you and Cousin Charley?" Ben volunteered. I knew he just wanted to get his hands on that camera. He loved working with gadgets, whether they made sounds or pictures or even toast. If something whirred, hummed, scratched, clicked, popped, heated, or produced an image, even a grainy, fuzzy one that rolled sideways as all television pictures did from time to time, he wanted to take it apart. Ben just seemed to have a knack for getting things to work the way they were supposed to work.

"Why, sure!" Eva handed the Brownie Hawkeye to Ben and showed him how to aim and what button to push. "Come here, Bunny," she said to Cousin Charley, who promptly left his dark brown, vinyl recliner to pose with her. He gave her a tight squeeze around the waist and a quick kiss on the cheek. Ben snapped the picture at just that moment.

"That'll be a good picture." Mama said what I was thinking.

"But we weren't even looking at the camera," Eva argued, even though a pleased blush still lingered on her face. I noticed that Cousin Charley's right hand had slid down over her hip and was gently massaging the bottom of her butt. The way she was smiling, I thought it must have felt really good. I also thought that my mama would never let daddy touch her like that in front of other people. But she had once let someone else touch her like that, I remembered, and quickly looked away.

"My best pictures are the ones that are taken of my back side," daddy cackled. We chuckled with him, remembering that he had once posed for a picture by bending over backwards, his face between his legs, just as the picture was taken. It was a blur of a butt.

Ben asked if there were other pictures that Eva would like to have taken today. "Yeah, let's get one of Bunny and me with your mama and daddy. The four of us haven't had a picture taken together for a long time," she said.

"Where do you want us?" mama asked, glancing around the room as she passed Bug to me. Mama was a skinny lady, but she had a pretty oval face and a dazzling smile that always made her look good in pictures. Rarely did she hesitate to step in front of a camera.

"How about on the couch?" Cousin Charley had taken a seat there beside daddy on the sturdy, modern sofa that matched the upholstered chair used in our family picture. Beige upholstery, beige walls, beige curtains, beige carpet. Except for a painting that hung over the fireplace, that dark brown recliner Cousin Charley always sat in, and some red, yellow, and green plastic flowers, this tiny living room was beige. I thought it was about the prettiest living room I'd ever seen.

Ben looked through the viewfinder before running a hand through his thin, brown, wavy hair. "No. That mirror over the couch will reflect the flash bulb. It'll mess up the shot." He walked around the rectangular mahogany coffee table, stopping to examine the possibility of posing four somewhat average-sized adults in front of the fireplace, in front of the picture window, or in front of the archway that led to the hall. None of these locations seemed to meet his approval.

"How about standing outside on the front steps? I can line you up out there before I shoot you." Ben punched me in the shoulder on his way out the door. "Did you get that?" he giggled. I stuck out my tongue and waved at him with my index fingers just as I heard a click and saw another flash. Ben had taken what would be an awful picture of me. Serves him right, I thought.

All the adults and Ben went outside to take more pictures while I stayed in the living room entertaining Bug. He made a pest of himself, pulling my nose, trying to pry open my mouth, and sticking his fingers in my ears. Those explorations would have made some funny photographs.

Soon the picture taking was done and we were all piling into Cousin Charley's car for the ride out to Great-Aunt

Alice's. I loved car rides, especially in nice cars like Cousin Charley always drove. His cars were always new, always comfortable, like this red and white '56 Chevy with big, chrome bumpers and some fancy chrome trim down the sides. Cousin Charley had washed and waxed the car on Saturday. He had vacuumed the floor mats, polished the dashboard, and sprayed something inside that smelled like men's aftershave. It reminded me of the commercial about the Aqua Velva man. Cousin Charley didn't smoke in his car, nor did he allow anyone else to contaminate the air with cigarette smoke. We weren't even allowed to chew gum in Cousin Charley's car.

When I rode in his car, I felt like a princess. I sat in the middle of the red fabric-covered backseat and imagined myself on a throne, riding in a parade. In my mind I was wearing a gorgeous white evening gown made with yards and yards of pure silk and waving a white-gloved hand to an adoring crowd who lined the streets waiting for a glimpse of me.

"Cousin Charley, if I ever do anything really special, like getting married, will you drive me to church in your fanciest car?"

He caught my eye in the rear view mirror, winked at me, and promised that he would indeed be my chauffeur, provided I would wait about ten years. I said, "It's a deal!"

I loved seeing the scenery as we drove through the city and out into the countryside. As I looked at the houses we passed by, I wondered what it would be like to live in some of them. I wondered if the people in them were happy. I wondered what kinds of jobs they had, or if they had any jobs at all. Some of them probably worked at DuPont or one of the furniture factories in Martinsville.

Others probably worked in Dan River Mills or at one of the garment factories. There were all sorts of factories around Martinsville and Danville.

I thought I might like to go into some of those factories someday, just to see what they made and how they put it together. The idea of working in a factory did not appeal to me, but the potential for making some money surely did. Some of those factories stunk to high heaven. If I had my choice, I'd rather work in a school or a library where people teach and study in a clean environment that smells good, except for all the stinky unwashed bodies of students like us without indoor plumbing. If I had my way about it, there would be a place at school for poor kids like me to take a bath every day. I hated feeling dirty.

Once out of the city limits, we started to see farm houses similar to ours—white, rectangular weather boarded structures built on rock foundations with a wide front porch, a wooden door in the center, and a couple of windows on each side. There would be a few windows on the second floor too, and a tin roof, usually painted apple green. If the owners had put in a bathroom, there might be a one story lean-to built off the back of the house. Some of them had an unpainted wooden outhouse situated far enough from the main house to provide privacy while keeping the fumes downwind.

I wondered if the people in these houses were good Christians. I could tell if they shared mama's belief that cleanliness was next to Godliness by the way they kept their yards and front porches. Some homes had lawns that had been recently mowed, with pretty pink and purple petunias blooming in baskets and painted green metal lawn furniture on the front porch. I knew it was wrong to covet what someone else had, but the words popped out of my mouth before I could stop them.

"I want *that* house." I pointed to an especially nice brick ranch-style house with huge magnolia trees, broad limbed maples, lots of boxwood, and all kinds of smaller shrubs, and flowers. There was even a rope swing with a wooden seat, just the kind that I loved.

"Uh-huh. Maybe by the time you are grown, those people will want to sell it to you," Eva nodded her head in agreement. "It sure is pretty."

"Probably costs a pretty penny, too. I doubt you'll ever have enough money to buy a house like that. No need to get your hopes up, trying to get above your raising," mama added.

Her negative outlook wasn't going to keep me from dreaming. "I'm not going to marry a farmer, that's for sure. I'm going to get a good job and make enough money to buy my own house." Mama ignored my comments and resumed her conversation with Eva, talking across me as if I weren't even there. Daddy looked at me with sad eyes that made me feel bad about what I'd said. "I love you, daddy, but I don't like farming," I whispered.

As we whizzed past the houses, all the blending of colors reminded me of a gadget that we had at school—a kaleidoscope. I realized that what I was seeing was a kaleidoscope of humanity represented by the houses we were passing. Some of the homes had overgrown weeds hiding tin cans, rusty farm equipment, plows, rakes, and other debris in the yard. Others had log barns nearby, emitting the sweet, unmistakable scent of tobacco being cured. That pleasantly fragrant smell was the only good thing about growing tobacco.

One house had an old, plaid, upholstered sofa sitting on the front porch and a dilapidated car perched on cinder blocks under a tree in the side yard, next to a pile of worn-out tires. A pile of firewood and an outhouse could be seen farther to the backside of the unpainted farmhouse. You could guess that the porch probably had rotten boards you could fall through if you weren't careful.

It seemed to me that there ought to be some laws about the way people maintained their homes. I knew I wouldn't want to live near one of those trashy ones if I had a really nice place. Doesn't it say somewhere in the Bible that we ought to keep ourselves and our surroundings in good order, that we honor God by taking good care of all that he has given us? I wondered if those homes were filled with people who were keeping secrets from each other. I wondered if one of them might have a girl my age who hadn't been saved yet.

Lost in thought again, I missed much of the conversation until I heard everybody laughing.

"What's funny?" I asked.

"You are Darla Mae. Your feeble mind just wanders around all over the place while the rest of us are talking about the newest car on the road." Ben had a habit of always needling me about something.

"I think about serious stuff when I tune *you* out," I told him. "Now what was everybody laughing about?" This time I looked at Eva whose warm smile always made me feel loved.

"Edsels," daddy answered. "That new car, the Edsel. The one with that strange-shaped front grill. I told Charley that it looked to me like a horse collar. He said,

'No, it looks like a toilet seat.' Then your mama said we ought to get one for the outhouse!"

"Two," Ben said, "since we have a two-seater." They laughed some more, but I didn't think it was all that funny. As far as I could tell the '58 Edsel was just one big, ugly car that was never going to have any impact on my life, now or in the hereafter.

Who cares about Edsels? I was thinking about whether I could talk to Cousin Charley about my secrets and all that was weighing heavily on my mind. When would I ever be able to unload this burden?

Chapter 12

"Is that Trickem?" Cousin Charley asked as we approached a tall, skinny man walking on the side of the road.

"Yeah, that looks like him, all right," daddy replied as he leaned out the open window of the car to call out to the man who was known to everyone in the MacKenzie community.

Trickem wasn't his real name, of course. Somebody gave Clyde Hanks that name a long time ago because he was always playing tricks on people. Daddy had warned us about Trickem when we were very young. "If somebody knocks on the door and there is nobody there when you answer it, you can bet that Trickem is hiding behind those boxwood bushes by the corner of the house. He wants to see what you'll do about that burning paper bag he's left on the front porch. You'd best not stomp on it. It's probably full of dried cow manure."

Trickem had been known to take live snakes to school to put in the teacher's desk, and sometimes used them to scare girls into climbing trees just so he could look up their skirts. I didn't know any of this firsthand, since Trickem was much older than Ben and me. He was probably about thirty, maybe thirty-five now. I just knew about him because mama and daddy would talk about him from time to time, always about some trouble that he was into.

"Hey, Trickem! Where you headed?" Cousin Charley slowed the car to a crawl before pulling over on the shoulder and coming to a stop.

"Oh, nowhere in particular. I'm jus' out for a Sunday stroll," Trickem drawled after he removed a lighted cigarette from his mouth and leaned down to peer into the car window next to daddy.

"You been doing all right?" mama asked. She was always asking people about their health, which usually gave her an opportunity to share some of her own aches and pains with them.

Trickem stood up, took a puff on his cigarette and flicked some ashes off it before answering, "Oh, yeah, I've been fine." A pleased grin tugged at the corners of Trickem's thin lips. "The po-lice took me to jail last Wednesday, and I just got out yesterday."

"What in the world for?" Mama couldn't contain her curiosity. Like everybody else in the neighborhood, mama knew that Trickem was often in trouble with the law, usually over something minor such as being drunk in public and resisting arrest. I noticed that Eva was squirming in her seat, trying to avoid the cigarette smoke. I could tell that she didn't like Trickem at all.

I was all ears, though. I wanted to have something else to think about that night, something besides those secrets I had been carrying around. Trickem usually told funny stories that daddy said were too "colorful" for children. Maybe that's why I liked listening to him. If anybody could get my mind off my troubles, it would be him.

Trickem removed a baseball cap lined with a week's worth of sweat rings and slapped it against his khaki work pants, a bit of red road dust flying off toward the car. "Well, they said I was causing a dee-stur-bance down there at Russell's Store," Trickem said with a laugh. "Hee-hee-hee hee! Oh, yeah, I caused a dee-stur-bance all right. Did it on purpose!" His long, lanky body folded almost double as he laughed again.

Ben and I were sitting on the edge of our seats, laughing along with him. I liked listening to Trickem talk because his words sometimes seemed like another language. He had trouble with some words that started with "ex," for example. He'd pronounce them "heck," as in "Heck-scuse me." If a word started with "ig," he'd pronounce it "Hick," as in "hick-nore." Then there were the words that he'd say with the emphasis on the wrong parts, like dee-stur-bance and po-lice. I could feel my ears bending forward to catch every word of this story.

"Yeah, I'd been trying to get me a ride to Chatham. Wanted to see my wife, my Sweet Sue. You know she's been working over there at the 29 Diner and staying with her mama since the old woman got so forgetful. Poor thing can't even remember what day of the week it is."

Sweet Sue's marriage to Trickem was an on-again, off-again situation. She'd leave him for months at a time, usually when he was drinking and getting into trouble. Eventually, she'd come back. You'd see her old car rambling down the road with Trickem sitting beside her, looking proud as a peacock.

Trickem took a drag off his cigarette and continued the story. "Well, nobody seemed to be going to Chatham.

I even offered to pay somebody to take me, but nobody seemed to have the time, so I got ole man Melton to drop me off at Russell's Store. I told him if I went in there and created a dee-stur-bance, they'd call the po-lice and the po-lice would take me to Chatham. When they let me out of jail, I'd be where I wanted to be. Hee-hee." His laughter was high and shrill.

All of us remained silent. I wondered if he was going to tell us what he actually did to get arrested, when he continued, "Yes sir, I staggered in there like I'd been on a binge, knocked over some stuff, got in an argument with ole man Russell, who accused me of showing my ass. I told him to keep looking; I'd sure enough show it. I turned around and started to unbuckle my belt when Deputy Sytes walked in. Well, he's taken me in enough times to know me. He said, 'Trickem, what are you up to today?' I knew this was as good a chance as I was going to get, so I told him I was just about to show my butt. Then I went ahead and dropped my pants. Whoo-wee! Y'all ought to have seen his face. Ole Mrs. Russell's, too. Good ole Deputy Sytes hauled me out of there and on to Chatham, just like I knew he would. Charged me with hin-decent heck-sposure. Hee-hee-hee."

Mama's face was beet red. Eva was hiding her face in her hands. I saw daddy roll his big gray eyes at Cousin Charley, who was biting his lower lip.

Trickem's story was funny. I wanted to laugh out loud but I knew that mama and daddy were embarrassed and would be even more embarrassed if they thought I found Trickem's story amusing. Ben peeked over the back seat and rolled his eyes. I looked at him and both of us clapped our hands over our mouths to keep from bursting out laughing. Eva had her arms folded across her chest and was looking straight ahead. She had heard all she wanted to hear.

"Bunny, we need to be going," she stated, her voice demanding immediate action.

"I'd offer you a ride but you can see I've got the car full," Cousin Charley said to Trickem as he started to pull away. Trickem was still laughing between puffs on his cigarette, which had burned down to the filter.

As soon as the car had moved away from him, everybody in the car started laughing, even Eva. "Can you believe that man?" she asked of no one in particular.

"Can you imagine poor Mrs. Russell witnessing such a thing?" mama asked, her face still scarlet.

"That man's not right in the head," Cousin Charley declared.

Daddy carefully shifted Bug from his right knee to his left. "That Trickem has been nothing but trouble since the day he was born." While Bug bounced and squirmed, daddy continued, "He was helping me with the hay a few years ago when he got to talking about his days in school. He said that he'd dropped out of school because hick-no-rance is heck-spensive, but he reckoned he could a-ford hit," daddy said, imitating Trickem's speech pattern.

"Expensive is what it has been for his daddy," Cousin Charley observed. "His poor mama worried herself to death years ago, and his daddy has spent just about every cent he ever earned bailing Trickem out of jail. What do you reckon happened to that boy?"

"I heard he was dropped on his head when he was a baby," Eva volunteered.

Ben decided to join the discussion. "Somebody said there was an eclipse the night he was born. The whole world got dark. And it was Halloween. Some people think witches stole part of his brain."

"Now son, who ever told you such a thing?" daddy asked.

"I heard it at school. Lots of kids mimic Trickem, you know." Ben seemed to be eager to defend himself.

I wanted to hear daddy's reply. "What he told me was," daddy cleared his throat before continuing, "when he was in school, it seemed to him that the other kids had brains that cruised along like Cadillacs, and his was just pedaling along on a bicycle." Daddy and Cousin Charley looked at each other and chuckled.

"Pedaling along on a bicycle. Hmm… that is a good one. I'll try to remember that, maybe use it in a sermon sometime. That ole boy may be smarter than we give him credit for being." Cousin Charley turned down a gravel road that was lined on both sides with tobacco fields.

"He's not as stupid as he wants people to believe," mama said. Her face was getting back to its normal color. "I think that because he was the baby in his family, he got pampered all the time and just didn't grow up right. He ought to be ashamed of himself."

"He certainly ought to be ashamed of himself today, telling that story in front of the children," Eva fumed, her arms crossed rigidly over her ample chest.

"I don't 'spect he has ever considered how other people are affected by the things he says and does," daddy commented.

"Well, he is one of God's children, too. There's some good in him somewhere." Cousin Charley seemed to rely on his role as a minister to steer us away from being judgmental.

"Is what Trickem did a sin? Would his mama have lived longer if he had behaved himself and honored her like the Bible tells us to do?" I asked.

"Sis, you ask some of the dumbest questions!" Ben glared at me over the back seat.

I made a face at him, sticking out my tongue in a most unattractive, immature fashion. "I do not ask dumb questions."

"Now Ben, Darla Mae's question is a good one," Cousin Charley said. "The Bible does tell us to honor our fathers and our mothers that their days on this earth may be long. I think Trickem's mother died of a heart attack. We have to believe that God wanted to take her to heaven when he did, otherwise she would be living today." He paused a moment to clear his throat. "If Trickem had stayed out of trouble the way his brothers and sisters did, his mother would have had a more pleasant life, maybe even a longer one." Cousin Charley seemed to relish this opportunity to work God into our conversation. I guess that was normal. He was a preacher after all.

"Well, if there's a good side to everybody, I hope Trickem soon finds his." Daddy glanced over his shoulder at Ben and me. "I've used Trickem's predicaments as an example with these young'uns. I've told them time after time that it's easier to stay out of trouble than it is to get into trouble and try to get out again."

"And I've told them that I might help them once if they make a mistake, but if they make the same mistake again, they'll just have to live with the consequences."

Mama gave me a whack on the leg when she saw me pinching the back of Ben's neck.

Ben gave me a smug look that said, "You got in trouble, but I didn't. Ha! Ha!" I couldn't do anything but glare at him.

Something in a tobacco field had caught daddy's eye, causing a turn in the conversation to a subject that I found utterly boring, so I slid back in the seat and let my mind drift to the future. Would I always honor my mother and father? Would they grow old, or would I be so bad that they'd want to die young? It seemed to me that Trickem was always happy, laughing, and having fun. Was it really so awful to be like that? I was right in the middle of my thinking when we pulled into the driveway of a really old farmhouse, where Great-Aunt Alice lived. I'd have to put my thinking aside while we visited with her.

Chapter 13

*C*ousin Charley stopped on a bare patch of ground under a row of maple trees whose branches created a cool canopy. He tooted his car horn three short blasts to announce our arrival at his mother's house. "That's my usual beep," Cousin Charley chuckled. People out in the country often blew their horns that way in case the home-owners were out in the garden or somewhere on the farm, so they'd hear the horn and know to come to the house—or hide, if it was someone they didn't want to see, like a salesman or someone trying to get them to attend a differ-ent church.

A short, frail, gray-haired woman pushed open the screen door leading onto her wide-planked porch and squinted into the bright sunlight. "Charley? Is that you, Charley?" Her voice was astonishingly deep, nasal, sound-ing like it came from the bottom of her feet.

"Yeah, ma, it's me. You need to wear your glasses so you can see me before I sneak up on you." He teased her before giving her a gentle hug.

"Who's that you got with you?" she asked as she looked up and saw all of us approaching the rickety wooden steps that led to the porch.

"Eva, of course, and that's Walter and his wife and children." Cousin Charley stepped aside and let his mother walk past him out onto the porch that ran along the side of the house.

"Eva, dear Eva, sweet thing, did you bring me a lemon chess pie today?" Great-Aunt Alice literally jumped up and down like an excited little kid, definitely not like an old woman—an old woman who was not wearing a bra! Her boobs jiggled just above her waist when she grabbed Eva. She warmly hugged her daughter-in-law and moved on to greet us before Eva could answer. It seemed like she had been waiting for a long time to see some company. When a person gets old, lives alone, and has no car or any way to go anywhere, I think her company could probably come from outer space and she would still be happy to see them. At least, Great-Aunt Alice seemed that thrilled to see us.

"Walter, it's so good to see you!" She grasped his right hand and squeezed it hard. "And you brought your wife—Irene, is it? And your children." Great-Aunt Alice's wide, toothless grin beamed at us from a deeply lined and darkly tanned face that reminded me of pictures I'd seen of trolls. "I didn't know you had but two. Have y'all had another one since the last time I saw you?" Great-Aunt Alice held out her arms to take Bug from mama.

"I'm Alene, and this is Doug, our youngest, but we call him Bug." Mama held him up for Great-Aunt Alice to take. Ben and I stepped aside, accustomed to having people make a fuss over Bug while seeming to forget that we were even around.

"Cute little fella," she said as her beady brown eyes studied his face. "Who does he take after?" She quickly scanned my parents' faces. "Doesn't look much like you or Walter, does he?" Bug grabbed her thumb and was trying to bring it up to his mouth.

"No, not much. He's going to be the best looking one of the bunch," mama said, her lovely face as radiant as I'd ever seen it. I wanted to scream, "But you didn't want him. You didn't want this baby!" Instead, I tried to keep my hatred for my mother from clouding my face.

"Y'all come on in the house," said Great-Aunt Alice, who carried Bug inside to a surprisingly cool room that doubled as a living room and kitchen. The adults started chattering away, bringing Great-Aunt Alice up to date on everything that was going on in their lives, how all the other extended family members were doing, how many kids some of the relatives had, and when they'd seen or heard from this one or that one. Listening to them was like hearing a broken record. Same old stories over and over again, mind-numbing repetition and very little of interest to me. To amuse myself I decided to examine the room and memorize every detail of it so that I could write about it in my diary that night.

Aunt Alice's house was a bit unusual. There was a wood stove similar to ours occupying one corner of this dual-purpose room. A Hoosier kitchen cabinet, with its built-in flour bin and slide-out counter top, and a white porcelain sink sat side-by-side on the adjoining wall with a hammered tin-front pie safe nearby. In the middle of the room narrow wooden benches surrounded a large wooden table covered with a bright yellow oilcloth. An oil lamp, salt and pepper shakers, a stack of dishes, a tin can filled with eating utensils, and some quart jars of homemade preserves were gathered in the middle of the table.

In another corner of this rather large, dimly-lit space, there was a small sofa covered in almost threadbare wine-colored velvet, a floor lamp with a fringed shade, a small side table topped with a crocheted doily, and three straight-back oak chairs. Looking somewhat out of place on the opposite wall was a new console television, complete with extendable rabbit ears. Someone had already wrapped aluminum foil around them for better reception. Small double windows and the open door to the porch provided some natural light and allowed an occasional breeze to drift through the room, bringing with it the fragrance of freshly-mown hay from a nearby field. Bumble bees buzzed above the blossoms of a pale pink crepe myrtle near one of the open windows.

Great-aunt Alice's house was clean, well-organized, and decidedly functional. She might have been poor, but she definitely seemed to make the most of what she had. I examined a faded framed photograph on the end table and concluded it must be of her and her husband when they were much younger, perhaps when they first got married. A tiny can of snuff was sitting beside it, along with a pair of glasses and a dog-eared copy of a family bible. I wanted to open it to see what might be written inside the cover, since I knew that was how people in my grandparents' generation kept track of births, deaths, marriages, and such. Maybe I could take a peek while the adults were talking if I could figure out how to get from my seat on one of the wooden benches to the other side of the room without being conspicuous. It didn't appear that there'd be much opportunity for that, so I quietly asked mama if Ben and I could go outside and roam around.

Once outside, Ben pulled his transistor radio from his shirt pocket and turned the dial to his favorite rock 'n' roll station. They were playing "Rock Around the Clock" by Bill Haley and the Comets. The tune had a fast rhythmic beat that seemed to get into my head and stay there. It got me to thinking about how life was changing for me.

Now that my friends and I were almost twelve, we never played with dolls anymore. Sometimes we listened to records if someone was lucky enough to have a 45 r.p.m. record player and some of those wild, rocking tunes by Elvis Presley. I had seen him on the Ed Sullivan Show. He looked so handsome. I'd seen pictures of him, too, shaking his hips like he had bugs biting his butt. Whenever I heard his music, my feet would start tapping and my body would start jiggling like a bowl of nervous Jell-O. I wanted to get up and dance, which was exactly what I did, sometimes grabbing the nearest doorknob as my partner. Mama told me I looked stupid, dancing that way.

"Do you think the good Lord put you on this earth to dance with a doorknob?" she asked whenever she saw me shuffling my feet and twisting my skinny hips in time with the music.

"Probably not, but I don't care," I would tell her. The door would swing back and forth as I gyrated from side to side in rhythm with the beat. It just felt so good to move like that. This strange, warm sensation would start pulsing through my body, which made me happy all over. In fact, I felt a little wicked when I was dancing. Old Reverend Hardshell's words would flit through my mind oh so briefly. Then I knew, if this was one of the pleasures of life that I'd have to give up in order to be "saved," the Devil might as well claim me now!

"Ben, do you think the people at Cousin Charley's church ever listen to rock 'n'roll music?" I asked, even though I thought I knew the answer.

He gave me a sideways glance, pursed his lips, and closed his eyes like he was giving my question some serious thought. "My opinion and the law of averages says…" Ben paused, giving emphasis to the law of averages, which had become his favorite reference point (never mind that the "averages" were pure conjecture on his part). Then, grinning from ear to ear, he concluded, "Old folks—never. Young folks—every time they get a chance!"

"How about Sister Sarah?" I cackled, as I considered what a sight it would be to see that self-righteous old bitty listening to Elvis. "She can really move." I tried to mimic the way she walked down the aisle that morning, when she gave her boys a spanking, by shaking my booty and holding my hands in front of my chest and moving them up and down.

Ben howled with laughter. "Sis, you are bad!"

"The people at Healing Waters probably don't like Elvis' music, either. They probably wouldn't want Elvis in their congregation, unless he promised to stand still and sing "There will be peace in the valley for me someday…" I stopped imitating Sister Sarah and stood ramrod straight like I was a statue while I sang way off-key.

Ben couldn't stop laughing. I was having so much fun I had to continue, "Imagine ole Reverend Hardshell listening to 'Jailhouse Rock'."

"Or 'Blue… blue… blue suede shoes,'" Ben tried to imitate the way Elvis said "blue," like he was blowing the word out of his mouth, his lip curled up on one side.

Ben and I wandered around the backyard, bantering back and forth as we tried to outdo each other's wild imaginings, before coming to rest at a homemade wooden lawn chair. Someone had recently painted its high back, wide arms, and sloping seat with white enamel paint, the same as the rope swing seat nearby. I grabbed the swing and let my spirits soar with the ever-increasing heights I was able to reach. Something about being up there among the tree branches reminded me of a hymn that both of us liked.

"One bright morning when this life is o'er," I started to sing, trying to stay in tune and on key.

"I'll fly away." Ben switched off his transistor radio and joined me on the chorus.

"To a land where… will… no more," I hummed the parts when I wasn't sure about the words.

Ben continued to join in singing the chorus, his voice a rich warm baritone. We finished that song and sang, "Washed in the Blood," with Ben singing every other line. Our timing and tune-carrying seemed to be getting better, so we sang several more including, "Standing on the Promises," before repeating "I'll Fly Away."

I unleashed my inhibitions, letting the tempo flow and volume increase as I continued to sing, "I'll fly away, oh glory, I'll fly away!" I imagined the words being captured on the wind, being taken higher and higher, away from me, as the swing made its ascent.

Without any effort on my part to keep it going, the swing slowed to a point where I was barely moving by the end of the song. Ben's eyes caught mine and locked for a moment in a look that I couldn't read. All I knew was that Ben and I were having fun away from our parents' watchful eyes for a brief time when we could indulge ourselves in shared interests. Maybe the time was right for me to share my secrets with Ben, too.

"Darla Mae, Ben, y'all come in and get some lemonade," mama yelled from the porch. "Curses," I thought, "Just when I was about to finally talk about what I had seen and heard."

Obedient kids that we were, we ran to the house where Great-Aunt Alice poured freshly-squeezed lemonade and set out a plate of tea cakes, the kind that Grandma Deacons used to make for us. I watched her go into a bedroom, then return momentarily with an ice cube tray, to add more ice to our drinks.

"Where is your refrigerator?" I asked. Mama shot me an angry look that told me immediately I had embarrassed her by asking a nosey question.

"Why, honey, it's back there in my bedroom."

I could feel my face form a question mark as my eyes met Great-Aunt Alice's. "When they brought my new television, there was nowhere to plug it in out here, unless I moved the refrigerator. So it's back there in my bedroom. Keeps the food just as cold back there as it does out here, and if I get hungry during the night my ice cream is closer by," Great-Aunt Alice chuckled. All of us politely chuckled with her.

"I even keep my money in the freezer," she continued.

My eyes registered surprise, as did those of everyone else.

"If a man ever tries to rob me, he'd never think to look there." She patted me on the shoulder and dropped another cube of ice into my glass, which splashed as it emitted a *plop-clink-clink-clink*.

"Mama, if you don't beat all—hiding your money in the freezer," Cousin Charley teased his aging parent. "How about letting me take care of some of that *cold* cash?"

"Charley, you're a preacher. You beg for money from your congregation or from your life insurance customers. Not from me. I'm going to spend mine. Get me a bathroom put in here pretty soon! No more splinters in my…" She stopped for a moment, glanced at Ben and me, then said "back side. I guess that's clean enough."

Both of us giggled knowing that she could have said a curse word we had already heard once that day. The adults giggled too before daddy launched into a tale of the encounter this morning with the cattle and their cussing owner. Ben and I added our observations of the incident, editing our comments to remove all the vocabulary that we weren't allowed to use.

We finished our lemonade and cookies, bid our reluctant farewells, and headed back to Martinsville. My secrets were still my own. I wondered if there would ever be a right time, a right person, to listen to me.

Chapter 14

After a quick trip back to our house to take care of the animals and to check on the tobacco curing in one of our two barns, we were at Cousin Charley's church for the second time that day, getting a double dose of preaching, praying, and singing—enough to last for several more Sundays. My family wasn't what you'd call regular churchgoers. We just went to church whenever my parents took a notion to go, even though mama was a sanctified saved soul and member of Healing Waters Gospel Church. Twice to church in one day. We were about to set a record.

I hoped the next time would be a lot cooler than it was today. We were in the midst of the dog days of summer when the 90-something degree sun beat down on asphalt roads, causing waves of heat to rise from the pavement, shimmering in their haste to get away from the super-hot surface. Thick cumulous and stratocumulus clouds gathered throughout the day, raising hopes of thunder showers that might bring blessed relief from the drought, along with some cooler temperatures. Of course, they might also bring hailstones and high winds that would destroy tobacco crops. Farmers, who were huddled in small groups in the shadow of the church's narrow porch, lamented the effects of the lack of rain on their crops, gardens, and cattle.

"I'm gonna have to sell all my herd if we don't get some rain soon. There ain't gonna be enough hay to feed 'em through the winter," I overheard one of them say, the worry evident in his slumped stance.

"I heard some big dairy farmer over around Gretna was willing to pay five dollars a bale for hay, just so he could hold onto his cattle," another man said.

"Sure wish I had about a thousand bales to sell him," my daddy added, reaching into his left pants pocket and fidgeting with something. Most of the men around him nodded their heads in agreement as they also felt in their pockets for loose change or whatever it is that men reach for when they engage in serious conversation. They talked about how their farm ponds were drying up, forcing them to irrigate their fields less often, and how they prayed for a steady two-day soaker.

I scanned the sky, looking for some sign of an imminent storm, and thought about the mysterious ways of nature as I wandered around the church yard finally coming to a dark green park bench that someone had recently provided. It had a small brass plate that said:

Her memory lives on
In the hearts of all who loved her
Mabel Meadows
December 12, 1901–April 25, 1958.

"That's nice," I thought. "Maybe someone would remember Uncle Travis with a nice park bench or a new pew in his church. I will have to talk to daddy about that and ask if he and some of the other neighbors might want to build one for the church. Daddy could donate the tree. Some of the neighbors could help with cutting it down. One friend who was particularly good with woodworking could make the bench, others could paint it, and the rest could take care of getting a little brass plaque made for it. That would be a fine tribute to their neighbor and would let those who hadn't gone to the funeral do something to acknowledge Uncle Travis." Formulating this plan made me feel like I had done something for him, too. I was eager to discuss it with daddy, but thought I should wait until after church.

Sitting there in the shade of a mighty, ancient oak tree before services, I watched as some folks arrived, their old Ford pickup trucks crunching over the gravel and bouncing through the dry ruts of an ill-defined parking lot before coming to a halt right beside the church. Others came in almost-new 1957 Chevys, looking like somebody had spent part of their Sunday afternoon polishing the chrome and scrubbing the whitewall tires.

Sister Sarah arrived with her husband and two boys in their rusty, black '52 Chevrolet, one of the ugliest cars on the road with its humped up hood and sloping back, looking like some giant nasty insect that ought to be stomped. She opened the door and thrust her tree-trunk–shaped right leg outside. While holding onto the roof of the car with one hand, she heaved her broad bulk out of the car so that her rear end was hanging out in the air while her left foot was still inside the car. I thought she made a perfect target for a sling shot attack, but reminded myself that bouncing spit wads off a woman's butt was an activity best reserved for substitute teachers.

Sister Sarah balanced about two hundred pounds on her right leg, brought the left leg out, stood up straight, and turned to look right at me as if she had been able to read my thoughts. Worse yet, she started to walk right toward me. I'd had enough encounters with Sister Sarah to know I was in for some spiritual harassment.

"Well if it isn't Miss Darla Mae," she chirped. "You and your folks were here this morning. I've been meaning to talk to you again," she said as she ambled across the patch of grass and weeds to where I was sitting. "Don't you look sweet and innocent over here all by yourself?"

I didn't know how to answer that question so I just said, "Hot, isn't it?" thinking that a comment about the weather was something safe to say.

"Oh, Child, it's gonna be a lot hotter than this in hell, which is where bad boys and girls go. The ones that don't go to church regularly. You need to get your mama and daddy to bring you to church and Sunday school every Sunday if you know what's good for you," she went on as she plopped her huge self right down beside me on the little wooden bench. I could have sworn I heard the wood crack under her weight.

I wanted to get up and run. Before I could move, she grabbed my arm with her sweaty palm. I looked up at her enormous round, red face. Perspiration had already beaded up on her forehead and was trickling down the sides of her face, dripping off her chin.

"Sinners go to hell, Darla Mae. You know what it means to be a sinner, don't you?" Sister Sarah asked as she pushed her pop-bottle thick glasses back on her broad nose, her hazel eyes staring right into mine. Humidity left limp strands of red hair hanging from the bun at the base of her neck.

"I—I duh… da… don't think I'm much of a sinner yet. I've only broken three commandments that I know about," I blurted out, feeling very unsure of myself. My own sweat glands were working overtime now. I looked away, toward the church door where a couple of men were still standing around talking. Daddy was no longer there.

"You will be committing more sins soon enough if you don't get your life right with the Lord. It's high time you did that. You will soon be twelve, responsible for every sorry thing you do," she declared, squeezing my arm a little harder. "I know girls like you. Little miss goody two-shoes. Make all "A's" in school. Participate in clubs, plays, and everything. Think they can do no wrong." Her voice was menacing, almost evil. She spat out the words the way boys my age spat out watermelon seeds. I wanted her to shut up.

"They do plenty that's wrong," she said, digging her fingernails into my skin. "God will make them pay." She glared at me, then let go of my arm to wipe sweat from her chin.

Free of her grip, I hopped up and ran toward the church, toward sanity. Or was it any saner inside than out there with Sister Sarah? I wondered.

"…Burn in Hell!" She called after me as I escaped into the sanctuary.

Knowing Sister Sarah had to go to the choir loft was a relief. At least maybe she couldn't hassle me anymore tonight. "That self-righteous old biddy," I thought. "Why does she badger me? I haven't done anything to her. What makes her so determined to save my soul? She ought to be paying attention to her own kids."

Inside the little white clapboard church with its clear glass windows, the air was stifling, steamy hot. There was no air conditioning, not even an electric fan. On this night the windows were open wide, but very little breeze stirred in the pine trees nearby. Moths and mosquitoes flitted in and out, attracted to the lights.

Throughout the church, worshippers were fanning themselves with cardboard fans which had a picture of Christ on one side and an advertisement for Scott's Funeral Home on the other. The acrid stench of sweaty humanity mingled with Evening in Paris perfume, Aqua Velva aftershave lotion, and marigolds that someone had arranged for the altar table. My parents and brothers were seated in a pew near the middle of the church. They'd saved me a seat, which I gratefully sank into as I tried to get a grip on my anger and wildly racing heart. Ben flapped his fan at me several times, bending the handle that looked like a tongue depressor for a horse.

"Where have you been? Are you OK?" Ben whispered just before Cousin Charley signaled the pianist to begin tonight's service.

"Yeah, I'm OK… tell you later," I whispered back as the pianist started to play "I'll Fly Away." We stood up to sing. Even though I often can't carry a tune in a bucket, I still try to make a joyful noise unto the Lord. Singing makes me feel good, the way it did this afternoon. After my encounter with Sister Sarah, I needed to do something to make myself feel better.

Ben was singing, too. I looked at him, caught his wink, and knew that this song had special meaning for us that had nothing to do with church. "One glad morning…" but not when this life is over, I thought. More like when it really begins. Look for Ben and me flying away in a supersonic US Navy jet.

My mind kept wandering in and out of Cousin Charley's sermon. At one point he looked up, gesturing toward heaven, when a little bug of some sort dropped down from the bare bulb lighting the pulpit. It fell right into his open mouth. I watched as the bug fell, then almost laughed out loud when Cousin Charley swallowed that bug, his Adam's apple bulging momentarily while he kept right on preaching. He'd always said that he didn't like to eat before he preached, that he just couldn't preach on a full stomach. I wondered if God had sent this little bug to give Cousin Charley something to tide him over 'til after the service. Or maybe God was just tired of hearing him say "Uh."

Cousin Charley was very fond of that word. His sermons always followed a sing-song pattern, "And God… uh… said… uh… to Moses… uh…" I couldn't decide if he was having trouble remembering his sermon or if he just wanted to stretch it out.

Maybe I'll ask him about all those "uh's" sometime. Maybe not, but I would like to ask him about the bug. How did it taste? And how come he didn't just spit it out?

On this night he was preaching a sermon about the Ten Commandments. I'd memorized them all long ago and understood most of them, except for the one about not committing adultery. What was adultery anyway? How would I know if I had committed that sin? I didn't even know what the word meant. A-d-u-l-t-r-y. It has "adult" in it, so it must have something to do with grown-ups. And it has "try" in it. So what could be sinful about adults trying to do something? Then it occurred to me—there is only one "t" in it, and there is an "e." A-d-u-l-t-e-r-y. An "e" for "evil," perhaps. That must be the bad part—adults trying to do something evil.

I decided to someday ask mama what adultery was all about. If she thought I shouldn't know, she'd use her favorite line, "That's for me to know and you to wonder about." Mama seemed to like having knowledge that she didn't have to share with an almost-twelve-year-old. I found that response incredibly annoying.

Perhaps I should ask daddy. He would say, "Go ask your mama." That's what he always said when he thought his answer would get him in trouble with her. I wondered then if all parents were this secretive, this contrary, before concluding that they must be since my friends had little luck getting their parents to answer their questions either.

My best bet would be to ask Betty Benson, who lived up the road from us. She was a couple of years older than Ben and seemed to know a lot about stuff that my parents wouldn't tell me, like where babies came out. I just wanted to know how they got in there in the first place! Betty told my friend Sally and me that babies were made by magic, the same as cows having calves and dogs having puppies. She said the man waves a magic wand over the woman and "Abra cadabra," a baby is made. I thought there was more to it than that.

My mind sure was wandering through this sermon. Cousin Charley said something about not using the Lord's name in vain. Now, I fully understood that commandment. Just the other day, I said something that I had overheard one of daddy's friends say, thinking I was being very grown up, talking like an adult. Mama and I were walking back from the mailbox when I said it. She turned to look me square in the eye and told me I was never to say that again. Then she broke a branch off a nearby forsythia bush and whipped me with it. She whipped me so hard I had little red welts on my legs with blood coming out of some of them. I promised right then and there that I would never take the Lord's name in vain again. Ever! That's why I wouldn't repeat what I said, not even in my diary.

I looked up when the choir started to sing "Love Lifted Me," only to see Sister Sarah staring straight at me as she sang, "I was sinking deep in sin, far from the peaceful shore, very deeply stained within…" God probably wouldn't want us to sit in a house of worship and be angry with someone else who was attending the same services, but at this very moment I felt a lot of anger toward Sister Sarah. If she only knew how independent I was, she would know that I couldn't be forced to do much of anything, especially to join a church whose beliefs I did not share, especially the one about women having to do whatever man says. My parents weren't trying to force me into anything. What gave her the right? Cousin Charley hadn't even tried to talk me into joining his church, although he did occasionally discuss daddy's salvation with him.

Cousin Charley said a few more words about following God's commandments before asking the congregation to stand for the closing prayer.

"If there is anyone… uh… here tonight… uh… who has ever broken any of… uh… God's commandments… uh… and hasn't asked… uh… for forgiveness… uh… I invite him or her… uh… to come to the altar now. Kneel and… uh…

pray with me. God is a... uh... loving and... uh... forgiving God. He will... uh... forgive you... uh... of your sins."

I watched out of the corner of my eye to see if anyone was going to walk up to the altar. Three people did: one elderly man, whose homemade wooden cane thumped the hardwood as he shuffled toward the altar, one skinny young woman, who clutched a very young baby that I'd heard had no daddy, and Sister Sarah waddled down from the choir loft. Cousin Charley took each of them by the hand, whispered a few words to them, and led them to the altar where he knelt while the others stood, holding on to the altar rail. He started praying. Soon each of them started praying their own prayers. People throughout the congregation started praying, too. There were all these voices, some high and shrill, some soft like a feather, some loud and demanding, and some deep and raspy filling the air. I wondered how God could hear them all at once like that, but then I remembered that he knew what we were going to say before we said it. One of Mrs. Rivers' vocabulary words popped into my mind. Omniscient. God is omniscient, all knowing.

I closed my eyes and silently said a quick thank you for my family, for all the fun we'd had that day, and then asked for forgiveness for my bad feelings toward Sister Sarah. Instantly, my anger melted away. All around me the praying continued until it had reached a frenzied pitch. In my almost twelve years, many of them attending churches where Cousin Charley preached, I had never before heard people praying like this. I wondered what was happening here.

Suddenly it sounded like someone was tap dancing at the altar. Curiosity got the best of me. I had to look up. There gyrating around the altar was Sister Sarah, with her eyes closed and hands pressed together, pointing toward heaven. She was stomping her feet, moving in a circle, bouncing her big breasts and buns. I thought she might be having an epileptic seizure, like one of the girls at school sometimes had. Then she started talking in a language that I had never heard, talking in "tongues," as they say in that church. I strained to discern her words from those of others, amazed that she continued her pleas well beyond the time when everyone else had stopped praying. Most other people around me lifted their heads and sat in wide-eyed wonder, focused on this mass of transformed humanity who seemed instilled with God's Holy Spirit.

Witnessing this event was both frightening and amazing. I was mesmerized by Sister Sarah's chanting and captivated by the radiant glow that seemed to surround her. Inside, I was in emotional turmoil, feeling as if a powerful magnet was drawing me toward that altar. Maybe God was speaking to me, trying to save my soul. Did He want me to commit myself to Him while I was still young and relatively sin-free? I wanted to rush straight up to that altar and make that *serious* commitment right then, that very moment. I leaned forward, looked to either side, and contemplated whether I could get past my parents and brothers without stepping on anyone's toes. Like me, they seemed transfixed by Sister Sarah's peculiar behavior.

"Wait! You're too young. You don't know what you're doing," my parents' words echoed in my head. My own conscience reminded me that I did not agree with all of the beliefs and practices of this denomination. I grabbed the back of the pew in front of me to keep myself from moving. Could I promise to love and honor God in all that I did and in all that I said for the rest of my life? Could I forego all the material things that I wanted—the fun, the excitement, and the glamour that I craved? Did I have to give up all that I wanted in order to be a servant of God? I was wrestling with these questions, vacillating between a definite "yes" and a "probably not" as Sister Sarah continued her fervent prayers in a language that no earthling understood. Slowly her dancing stopped. She dropped to her knees and said, "Thank you, Lord Jesus," in plain English.

"Amen." Cousin Charley concluded the service and strode toward the back door as the pianist began to play "God Be with You 'Til We Meet Again." Sister Sarah stood up and followed him out the door, leaving the rest of us to disperse whenever and however we wanted. My family moved quickly and quietly out of the church, waving goodbye to Cousin Eva and stopping only long enough to shake hands with Cousin Charley.

Chapter 15

Raindrops began to fall as we exited the church, spotting the dusty ground around us, giving rise to an odor that can best be described as "fresh wet earth." Next to the sweet scent of a clean, freshly-scrubbed body, I've always been partial to this smell that I associate with summer rain. I stood outside the car inhaling deeply.

Mama looked skyward and said, "Thank you, Lord." I looked up too, allowing the cool, refreshing water to splatter over my face. Ben was beside me, mouth open, trying to catch some of the drops as they fell, the way we did when we were much younger.

"Y'all get in the car before you get wet," daddy ordered.

"Alene, are you going home with us?" he asked, noticing that she was still standing outside after Ben and I had folded down her seat and climbed into the back of the Dream Wagon.

"What? Oh, it is so wonderful to see this rain," she said, as she got into the car and took Bug from daddy. "I'm just so happy to see the rain."

Lightning flashed from sky to ground, setting off a series of thunderous rumbles. Normally, the sight of lightning so close by would have frightened me, but on this night it just fascinated me, the way Sister Sarah's prayers had. Bolts of lightning hurling from the sky like jagged exclamation points seemed to be a fitting end, a way of punctuating this eventful day.

"Looks like we might get what we've needed for so long," daddy said, his voice sounding more optimistic than I'd heard it in weeks.

"Do you think rain was what Sister Sarah was praying for? Do you think God answered her prayer that quickly?" I asked. Not wanting to miss a word of their replies, I slid forward so that I could hang over the back of mama's seat.

"Humph," Daddy snorted. "There is no telling what Sister Sarah was praying for. I bet she couldn't tell you herself!"

"Walter, you don't know what she was talking to the Lord about. For all you know, she might have been praying for you to see the light," mama said, rarely missing an opportunity to remind daddy about his unsaved soul.

"Humph," daddy said again. He started the engine, shifted the gears, and eased the station wagon back onto Highway 57 for our journey home. "Sister Sarah might as well save her breath for when she's ninety years old and might need it."

"I'll bet she was praying for your sorry soul, sis." Ben tapped me on the shoulder with his knuckled fist.

"Probably yours," I said, glaring at him in the dark. "But why was she tap dancing and talking in tongues?"

"You'll have to ask your Cousin Charley that one," mama said. "In all my years, I have never seen anything like that. Have you, Walter?"

"Can't say that I have," daddy answered without taking his eyes off the road. "I've heard Charley talk about it happening a few times. Don't know if he's ever got that carried away. I doubt it. He's not one to get too fired up, like some preachers we know."

"You wouldn't be talking about Reverend Hardshell, would you?" mama asked.

I slid back in my seat, but not before hearing my father mutter, "What do you think?"

Mama was quiet for a moment before changing the subject, "I think I'd like to sleep for two days, just to rest up from today." Mama yawned, cupping her right hand over her mouth.

Mama had just said what I suspect all of us felt. Exhausted, each of us seemed to sink into our seats. Silence enveloped us, insulating us with our individual thoughts. Mine were on the spectacle that I had witnessed and the words of Sister Sarah when she had grabbed me before the service. Tomorrow I would tell my parents about my encounter with Sister Sarah and how I had thought about joining Cousin Charley's church, but tonight I was too tired to discuss it.

I was hardly aware of our arrival home. Each of us engaged in our nighttime routines out of habit, with little thought and virtually no conversation other than the usual "good night, sleep tight." Before climbing into bed, I folded my hands together and offered another prayer of thanks for this unusual day in my life and asked God to guide me in all the decisions that I might need to make in the days and weeks ahead. Rain continued its rhythmic tapping against the tin roof of our house, so softly that it had the effect of a lullaby, gently enticing me to the splendid world of totally relaxed, undisturbed sleep.

Chapter 16

"Up and at 'em," daddy said as he pounded on the door to my room the next morning.

"I'm up," I answered, putting one foot on the floor just to be sure that I was telling the truth. An early riser, I was usually up soon after I heard my parents stirring downstairs, but this morning I moved so slowly, I felt like I had been tranquilized.

"Get moving, then! Y'all need to get your chores done before breakfast." I heard daddy's feet clunking on the stairs as he went down them. Ben's much lighter steps soon followed.

I quickly dressed in a pair of cut off dungarees and a sleeveless plaid shirt before hurrying downstairs to take care of feeding the chickens. Kati scampered along beside me, meowing loudly to remind me that it was time for her morning meal, too. Back at the house, I set the table for breakfast, changed Bug's wet diaper, and played with him until mama got the sausage, gravy, and biscuits on the table. I poured coffee for everyone, sat down, and added two heaping teaspoons of sugar to mine. Mama had long ago given up on getting us to drink milk.

"The coffee is good this morning," I confirmed after taking a generous sip.

"That's what you say every Monday morning," daddy chuckled, looked at me out of the corner of his eye, and winked. He and I had often talked about how mama's coffee went from good on Monday to bad on Tuesday to awful on Wednesday. "Stump water" is what he called the bitter, bad tasting Thursday version.

Mama had grown up during the Great Depression and had lived through rationing during World War II. Reusing coffee grounds and re-brewing tea were among the many ways that she made sure we'd always have plenty to eat and drink. If we couldn't plant it, raise it, or find it growing wild on our farm, we probably didn't eat it. The main exceptions to this rule were coffee and sugar. While we could use honey that we "robbed" from our bee hives to replace sugar in some foods, we had no options for coffee and tea. Our taste buds suffered after four days of brewing, but at least we were able to distinguish good coffee from bad.

"Your mama is trying to teach you the difference between right and wrong, and she's doing it with coffee." Daddy took a gulp and flashed a gap-toothed grin. "What's *right* always leaves a good taste in your mouth."

"And what's wrong will always be bitter!" mama added while spooning gravy over her freshly baked biscuits.

I studied mama's face for a moment and wanted to ask if she had ever had a bitter taste but decided I'd better not. Instead I said, "I wonder if Sister Sarah has a bitter taste in her mouth this morning," remembering what she had said to me last night.

"Now why would you say that after seeing her prancing around the altar last night?" daddy asked, his head tilted to one side. His steel gray eyes rolled in my direction, and his lips curled in a smirk.

I debated with myself about what to tell them before I dove right in. "Because she had a little talk with me before the service. Told me I'd better get my life right with God before I got any older. She said that people like me would burn in hell if we didn't join church and start attending regularly."

"So that's what was going on right before the service?" Ben speared another piece of sausage and took a bite.

"Yes. She about scared me to death. I had a hard time paying attention to Cousin Charley's sermon because I was so angry with her. She called me a little goody two-shoes. And she said just because I was a good student and involved in a lot of activities, I thought I couldn't get in trouble. She grabbed my arm and wouldn't let me go, until finally she had to wipe some sweat off her face. That's when I ran inside. I'm telling you, I was not feeling any Christian love for that woman." I took a quick sip of my coffee and continued before they could interrupt me. "But then, when she got to praying and talking in tongues and all, I felt like I was seeing a different person, someone almost like an angel or the Holy Spirit or something. I wanted to rush right up to the altar and get saved. Did y'all see how Sister Sarah glowed? Did y'all see the Holy Spirit? Or at least feel it?"

All three swung their heads around to look at me as if I were some ghostly apparition.

"Sis, you are too weird," Ben said, shaking his head from side to side.

Mama sat there staring at me, like she was getting madder by the minute. "Darla Mae, you listen to me and you listen good. That woman has no business telling you what you should or shouldn't do. She's no saint. I could tell you what a sorry, no-account slut she was when she was a teenager, but you don't need to know all that. You just ignore her from now on. If she says anything more to you, tell her she'll have to talk to me."

"Or me," daddy said, his eyes flashing a furious glint. "When and where you join a church is none of her business. Like I've told you before—there is a lot that goes on in a church that has nothing to do with worshipping God. As for living a righteous life, don't get me started on that!" Daddy shifted his gaze from me to mama and seemed to glare at her for a moment. "Some folks need to think about saving their own souls before they try to reel in anyone else."

I was shocked by their statements, but also relieved that I could put Sister Sarah out of my mind. "Okay. All right. I'll try to stay away from her. But if she says anything more to me, I'll just tell her to take it up with one of you," I promised as I rattled my coffee cup back into the saucer. My breakfast was getting cold, so I ate quickly, savoring the taste of all that was right in my life that day.

Chapter 17

*T*uesday began like any other day on the farm. All of us did our morning chores, discussed the tasks of the day over breakfast, and got busy taking care of them when we'd finished eating. Mama and I cleaned up the kitchen, made beds, and did the week's laundry, which we hung out to dry. Bug was content, occasionally shaking his rattler while squirming around in his playpen.

By late afternoon, daddy and Ben had gone to the fields down by the river to bale hay that daddy had cut on Monday. Mama and I went to the garden nearest the house to pick green beans, squash, and tomatoes. Mama had moved Bug's playpen outside under a big oak tree where he could take his afternoon nap within earshot. We had plenty of time to gather our vegetables before he would wake up.

Clods of clay broke under our feet as we selected yellow crookneck squash bleached white by the unrelenting August sun. Mama and I were picking wilted green beans when we saw daddy driving the tractor as fast as it could go, cutting across another hay field and heading toward the house. A man, who looked like Trickem, appeared to be holding Ben on the flatbed trailer daddy used to haul hay.

"Lordy mercy! Something has happened to Ben." Tears glistened in mama's eyes as she ran to meet the tractor, which daddy had stopped beside the garden.

"Ben, Ben," she cried. Mama turned his face toward her. She lifted one of his swollen eyelids with her thumb and index finger. Her face turned white. Her lips started to tremble. She began to stroke Ben's arm with her deformed thumb, rubbing it gently back and forth while mumbling something I couldn't hear.

"What in the world…?" I stared in horror at Ben's limp body covered with welts, which had formed and were still popping out on my brother's face, neck, arms, and chest.

"He's been stung," Trickem and Daddy answered simultaneously.

"A whole swarm of yella jackets," Trickem added. "I picked 'em offen him fast as I could." Trickem's voice quivered.

"Alene, get in the car. We gotta get this boy to the doctor before he dies," daddy ordered as he strode toward the station wagon with Trickem following close behind, carrying Ben in his arms. I wondered why Ben couldn't walk. Then I noticed that his left shoe was missing and his ankle was swollen.

"Shouldn't we take him straight to the hospital?" mama argued.

"Too many traffic lights. Too far. We can get him to old Doc Shoat's office a lot quicker than we can get to the hospital."

"Darla Mae, grab my handbag and get my car keys off the rack in the kitchen," mama said as she helped Trickem ease Ben onto the back seat. Mama climbed in after him.

"Bring baking soda and a wash rag," Trickem said. He was filling a bottle with water from the spigot at the side of the house. "We can dab some soda on those stings before we get to the doctor's office."

My mind shut down and my body must have been on automatic pilot because I had grabbed all four items and was back at the car in a flash. No time to think. No time to feel. Just had to do what I was told and hope that it was enough.

"Here," I offered the items to mama through the car window.

"You take care of Bug till we get back," she said, swallowing hard, the tears ready to roll at any minute.

"I will," I promised, trying to hold back tears of my own. "Bye Ben," I said, waving to him through the car window. He tried to open his eyes, but only managed to raise his lids enough for me to see a slit of his pupil.

"Step back, Darla Mae. Time's a wasting!" Daddy peeled out of the driveway, kicking up gravel, and disappeared down the road, leaving a trail of dust behind him. I stood there watching them until the car disappeared around a bend. Suddenly I felt so alone, an abandoned child with a brother who was facing an uncertain future.

"Dear God, please don't let Ben die," I prayed out loud. With those words, the dam straining to hold my pent-up emotions ruptured. Tears streamed down my face. They dripped off my chin, leaving little wet spots on my shirt. "If you'll just let him live, I'll dedicate my life to You. Soon. I will. I promise. And I'll tell Ben about my dreams. And my secrets. And everything. If you'll just let him live."

Sniffling wasn't enough to stop the flow of liquid from my head. I badly needed a handkerchief. Back in the house, I grabbed the first cloth that I saw, a clean diaper, and blew my nose. "What the heck," I reasoned. "It'll come out in the wash. If it doesn't, who cares? Right now, my older brother might be dying. He is more important than anything in the world to me."

Bug's shrieks, however, demanded my immediate attention. I rushed back outside, scooped him up from the playpen, and stood holding him tightly in my left arm while gently patting his back with my right hand. He must have sensed something was wrong because he continued to cry after I had fed, burped, and changed him. I rocked him back and forth as I sang a lullaby, making up the words as I went along.

Hush little Bug, now don't you cry.
You're Big Sis Darla's little sweetie pie.
Ben will be all right, now don't you cry
Mama and daddy will be home bye and bye.

Eventually he calmed down, allowing me to put him back into the playpen. Kati, who always seemed to sense when I needed a friend, ran between my legs, and rubbed her chin against them to signal her presence. My parents had only been gone for a few minutes but it seemed like hours already. A part of me wanted to sit there on that old metal lawn chair by Bug, cat in my lap, and surrender to all my thoughts and fears. Another part of me wanted to do something, anything, to keep myself too busy to even think about what might be happening to Ben.

I sure wished we had a telephone. If we had one, I could call the doctor's office to ask what was going on with my brother. Without one, all I could do was to stay here and wait until my parents came home. I wasn't alone for long.

Cousin Charley's shiny Chevy pulled into the driveway. He and Eva got out and walked slowly toward me, their faces all bright and smiling, their usual countenance. Kati leaped from my lap and ran toward the barn when she heard their footsteps.

"Hey, Darla Mae. Looks like you've got babysitting duty again," Eva said cheerfully.

"Looks like somebody left here in a hurry," Cousin Charley noted, stopping to check out the track left when daddy had spun out of the driveway. Daddy had always said Charley was one of the most observant people he'd ever known.

I looked up at them, my heart filled with relief that they were here. Tears sprang to my eyes once again before I could speak.

"Darla Mae, what's wrong?" Eva's voice registered immediate concern. She knelt beside me and wrapped an arm around me. I leaned into her, sobbing into the warm softness of her bosom.

"Ben may die," I blubbered, letting my tears flow unchecked onto her pretty pink blouse.

Cousin Charley knelt in front of me, gently took my right hand, and very calmly asked, "What happened?"

I wanted to look up at him, but I knew my face was red splotched and my nose was running. Between sobs, I told him all that I knew, which wasn't much. He handed me his fresh, clean monogrammed handkerchief.

"How long ago did they leave here?" Cousin Charley wanted to know.

"Half an hour, maybe an hour. I really don't know." I felt miserably inadequate with no sense of time and so few details.

Cousin Charley checked his watch. "It's five o'clock. They've had more than enough time to get to Doctor Shoat's office." His eyes seemed to search the ground between us, as if looking for a message in the blades of grass. When he looked up there was warmth and compassion in his eyes as he spoke, "Where can I find a phone around here?"

"Russell's Store,"

"OK. Here's what we're going to do. Eva is going to stay here with you while I go down to Russell's Store to make a call to the doctor's office. If I need to, I'll drive over to Chatham myself to see how Ben is doing. Before I go, let's have a word of prayer."

I closed my eyes, bowed my head, and tried to hear what Cousin Charley was saying. His words were whispered, mumbled, punctuated with "and... uh..." All I really understood was that Cousin Charley was asking God's mercy on all of us, and especially on Ben. "Amen," he said, and then let go of my hand.

I opened my eyes and felt a sense of peace sweep over me as I watched Cousin Charley drive away. Eva slid her arm from around me, stood, and stretched. She walked over to the playpen and looked down at Bug, whose sound sleep was interrupted by an occasional kick. Sadness washed over her face. "I remember when Ben was no bigger than Bug is now. He used to make the most awful fuss when he wanted somebody to pick him up." Then she blinked her eyes and straightened her shoulders.

"Darla Mae, why don't I help you take these clothes off the line? Maybe we can get them ironed, folded, and put away before your mama gets home. If we keep busy, the time will go by faster."

I looked up at her sympathetic blue eyes and thought how lucky I was that my daddy's first cousin had married such a sweet person. "OK," I said as I stuffed the handkerchief into the pocket of my denim shorts. "I'll get the clothes pin bag. Oh, I almost forgot about the vegetables. I need to take those in the house, too."

I picked up the basket filled with the world's best tasting tomatoes and took them to a table on the back porch. Eva brought the buckets filled with squash and green beans, which she sat down next to the tomatoes. "We'll deal with those later," she said.

We made several trips back and forth to the house with our week's worth of laundry, which we dumped on the bed in my parents' bedroom. I folded all our underclothes and put them away in their proper places. Eva pulled out all the pieces that needed to be ironed, which she proceeded to moisten with the sprinkler we'd made from a pop bottle and a lid with holes in it. She carefully rolled each piece and stuffed it inside a pillow case to "season" while we folded sheets, towels, dish clothes, etc. I put them away before going back outside to check on Bug.

He had rolled over and was trying to push himself up on his elbows. I picked him up and took him into the house where I sat him on the floor to play. Now I could be with Eva and take care of Bug at the same time. Eva had found the iron and ironing board, which she sat up in the kitchen in preparation for the task ahead.

"You just look after Bug. I'll do the ironing," she said as she took the first shirt from the pillowcase. "But first, would you get me some clothes hangers?"

I did as I was asked, settling down on the floor to play patty-cake with Bug. Later I entertained him with a finger puppet mama had made. He seemed more interested in chewing it than in listening to my puppet story. Eventually he wanted nothing more than to sit in my lap. I was happy to have someone to hold.

Together we listened to Eva humming hymns as she worked, rhythmically lifting and pressing the iron against fresh sun-dried laundry, sending up the odor of hot, wet cotton. It was the comforting smell of home and family. I wondered if heaven smelled like this.

When Bug went back to sleep, I laid him in his crib, stomach down, head to the side. He looked almost angelic.

"I'm finished," Eva announced. "Can you put these last pieces away?" she asked, handing me hangers with shirts belonging to Ben and me.

"Of course," I took them from her, ran upstairs, and quickly back down again, in time to see a shiny black '56 Ford pull into the driveway.

Mrs. Russell rolled her short, plump body out of the car and waddled toward the back door, carrying a casserole dish, a carton of soft drinks, and a beige straw handbag. The sight of her carrying food evoked a memory that caused intense pain in my chest, as if I had been slugged. My heart felt like it was crushed, unable to beat. The last time Mrs. Russell had come to our house bringing food was when Grandma Deacons had died. Now she must be coming to tell us about Ben.

"Do you know who that is?" Eva's question brought me back to the present.

"Uhhh, that's Mrs. Russell from the store," I told her through another rush of tears. "Ben must have…" I couldn't say it.

Eva must have had a sense of foreboding, too, since she suggested that I stay in the house with Bug while she went out to greet our visitor. I could hear some of their conversation through the screen door.

"Hey, I'm Eva Hill. Could I give you a hand with that?" she said as she reached for the casserole dish. "My husband Charley is Walt's first cousin."

"Well, Eva, your husband was at the store a little while ago, making a phone call about little Ben. He wanted me to get word to you about what's happening." She must have remembered that Eva didn't know who she was because she finally introduced herself. "Oh, Eva, I'm Claire Russell. My husband and I run a store down the road from here."

Both women lowered their voices, making it impossible for me to hear all they were saying. I caught a word here and there. "Ben… hospital… not breathing… shock…" Not knowing the rest of what they were saying was making me angry.

I went to the back door and said, "Why don't you come on in and tell me what's going on with my brother?"

Both women turned to look at me, their faces full of heartfelt concern. Together they approached the kitchen door, bringing food and soft drinks with them, which they sat on the kitchen table.

"I made a macaroni and cheese casserole today. Thought you all might like some for your supper tonight." Mrs. Russell looked at me and attempted a smile. Then she hugged me and said, "I think Ben's going to be all right. Doc Shoat gave him a shot and put him on an am-alance to send him to the hospital in Danville. He'd gone into some kind of shock, anti-something shock, the kind that people get if they're allergic to bee stings. She fumbled through the items in her purse before removing a scrap of paper, which she read before handing it to me.

"Ana-phy-lactic shock. Ben had been stung so many times all over his body that he had a really bad reaction. And he had trouble breathing. But they have him at the hospital now and they'll take good care of him. Don't you worry." She gave my shoulder a little squeeze before dropping her arm and stepping away from me.

"Oh, thank God!" I was so relieved to hear Ben was still alive that I started to cry again. This time Eva hugged me and assured me that we'd know more about Ben's condition when Cousin Charley returned, which wouldn't be until tomorrow morning. He had told Mrs. Russell that he would stay overnight at the hospital with my parents.

"Does that mean you're going to stay overnight with me?" I know my distraught face must have registered all the apprehension that I felt about staying by myself.

"Of course, I'm staying with you!" Eva's bright smile brought a hint of a smile to my face, too.

"Darla Mae, I'm going to call the hospital and ask to speak to your mama. If she has anything new to report, I'll come back to tell you." Mrs. Russell picked up her handbag and started towards the door.

"Thanks. We'd really appreciate knowing about any change. Thanks for bring us this food, too." I managed to remember my manners.

"Well, if you need anything more from the store, tell me now and I'll bring it right back to you. I brought those Dr. Peppers. Couldn't remember what kind y'all usually buy, but if you'd rather have some other kind, I'll bring them."

"Dr. Pepper is my favorite," I told her truthfully. "Thanks!"

Mrs. Russell's round face broke into a beaming, ear-to-ear smile that I'd seen many times in my life. We said our goodbyes and watched her leave before returning our attention to the food.

"Would you like something to drink? I'm a bit thirsty. I think I'll have one of those Dr. Peppers," Eva said as she took a glass from the cabinet over the sink and filled it with ice. "Do you want one?"

"Let's split one," I suggested, since I never drank more than half a soda at a time. We sat at the table sipping the sodas, watching the bubbles break on the surface. I thought about how rapidly my emotions had gone up and down today, like they'd been riding an elevator that was racing to the top floor and plummeting to the bottom. At this moment, it had stopped somewhere in the middle. Life was a little better. Ben was probably going to be all right. At least he wasn't dead. Then I remembered my bargain with God, my promise to dedicate my life to him if Ben lived. That serious commitment had seemed so easy to make when I thought Ben might die, but now that he was probably going to live, I didn't know if I could make it. But God would understand, wouldn't he?

I was happy that Eva was going to stay with me until my parents came home. We had something special for dinner that we didn't have to make ourselves. Enough was right in my world to breathe a sigh of relief.

Chapter 18

My thoughts were short-circuited when I heard ole Betsy, our black and white Holstein, bleating loudly. She needed to be milked right away. And not only that: the barn stall needed to be mucked, the hogs, dogs, and chickens needed to be fed, eggs needed to be gathered, wood needed to be brought in for the cook stove. Bug needed to be fed and bathed. Kati needed some food and fresh water, too.

I had been doing many of these chores for years, except for milking the cow. I found the whole process a little intimidating, especially when our cow was known to be uncooperative. She'd even tried to kick daddy once when he'd touched her teats with hands that were apparently too cold.

"I don't know how I'm going to milk old Betsy," I said to Eva, whose blue eyes grew wide. Apparently she realized one of us had to do it, but that it probably wouldn't be her.

"Can't you just skip the milking for tonight?" Eva asked. She was a city girl, born and bred—a woman who didn't particularly like animals. She didn't even have a house cat.

I stifled a giggle, not wanting to embarrass her. "Ole Betsy wouldn't like that. Her sac might rupture," I offered by way of explanation.

"Oh... umm... ahh... Do you think you can do it?" Eva asked.

I started to shake my head "no" when I saw her grimace. "Well, daddy is fond of saying, 'A man's got to do what a man's got to do.' If you can take care of Bug, I'll take care of the chores, including the milking," I said with all the confidence I could muster.

I took a deep breath, got the milk bucket from the pantry, filled it half full of water, and headed down the path to the stable. Old Betsy was hanging over the fence, bellowing at the top of her lungs. She watched me approach, staring at me with huge menacing eyes.

"Daddy's not here to milk you tonight," I said, thinking that my friendly tone of voice might convince her to be kind to me. She shook her head back and forth, stamped her feet and swished her tail. Her actions told me that she didn't like me, no matter how friendly I sounded.

I set my bucket down outside the stable door. Inside I took some hay from an open bale and put it into the hayrack. Old Betsy, being a creature of habit, moseyed on into the stall, lowing again loudly enough to scare me. Daddy had left a rope and halter there where he could tie old Betsy to the bin while he was milking her. I examined the apparatus, trying to figure out how I would get it over her head, before I concluded that old Betsy would have to stand still without being tethered.

I pulled up a short three-legged stool near the cow's udders, patted her rump the way I'd seen daddy do, and sat down to wash her teats. They felt firm, warm, and somewhat like the skin on my feet. Washing them was easy. Then I gripped one the way I'd seen my parents do, squeezed, and pulled it downward, aiming it toward the empty bucket. Nothing happened. I tried again and again, switching teats. Still nothing.

Old Betsy seemed to be getting a little annoyed with my feeble attempts. She turned sideways, lowered her head, and bellowed loudly in my left ear. I grabbed the milk bucket before she could kick it over. "Isn't it bad enough that I have to be in here smelling your sour breath and that cow patty you dropped outside the door?" I asked as I settled the bucket in place and tried again to squeeze some of that precious white liquid from her. Still nothing.

"I'm sorry," I yelled at her, "but you're just going to have to let me have your milk!"

"Can't talk her into giving it up?" a familiar male voice laughed as he poked his head into the stable. J.R. stood there surveying my efforts, a grin spreading across his handsome black face. I jumped, momentarily frightened by the unexpected presence of another person in the stable.

"J.R., I didn't know you were anywhere around here," I said. "I didn't hear you walk up."

Behind him another voice said, "I ain't never seen a woman who could milk a cow as well as a man." Trickem. In all the excitement of the last few hours, I had forgotten about him.

"Step aside, I'll take care of this old girl," J.R. said, as he expertly dropped the halter and rope over the cow's head. I gladly gave up my seat and went outside.

"Trickem, hey, I'm sure glad to see you." I was surprised by the complete sincerity with which I had spoken those words to the neighborhood rascal. "Are my parents home already?"

"Naw, they ain't home, yet." He shook his head sideways, causing a strand of light brown hair to fall across his forehead. He brushed it back with his left hand.

"Well then, tell me what happened. Is Ben going to live? Mrs. Russell told us he'd probably be OK, but I want to know for sure." I stared at him, trying to read the truth in his pale blue eyes.

He leaned across the fence, one foot parked on the bottom pole, and thoughtfully chewed on a piece of straw before answering. "What happened was—I heard the tractor going over in the bottoms and decided to walk over 'are to see if your daddy needed any help with loading the bales. Walt was driving the tractor while Ben threw the bales onto the trailer. For a little feller, he's pretty strong."

"Yeah, so what happened?" I was getting impatient.

"Well, I'm a getting to that. We was loading hay when all of a sudden, Ben started screaming. I looked over at him. He'd fallen over clutching his ankle. I think he'd twisted it, and he was covered up with yella jackets. Must a stepped in a nest of 'em. You know those little bastards, I mean devils, will keep stinging you, over and over again. 'Em and hornets are about the meanest insects there are. They don't bother me none, though. Guess I don't smell good to 'em," Trickem chuckled to himself. "I run over to Ben and started picking 'em yella jackets off of him as fast as I could. I scraped a whole passel of them off his head with my bare hands." Trickem showed me a few welts on his hands and arms. "I got a few stings myself, even got some on my face and neck here," he said pointing to one on his throat, "but they don't hurt me none."

"Your daddy stopped the tractor and told me to jump on the trailer with Ben. We headed to the house as fast as we could go. I finally got all the little devils offen him before we got out here. Ben had already started to break out in welts all over. His eyes was almost swole shut when we got here. Then your daddy drove like a bat outta hell getting to Chatham. On the way to the doctor's office, Ben started coughing and gagging. Old Doc Shoat took one look at him and his eyes about bugged out. You know he wears those glasses with the pop bottle lenses. You should have seen his eyes." He opened his own eyes wide, as if trying to mimic the doctor.

In spite of his comical appearance, I wanted to scream, "Just tell me about Ben," but I bit my lower lip and waited for Trickem to continue.

"Anyhow, he gave Ben a shot of something right away and had his nurse call an ama-lance. They took him to the hospital by ama-lance 'cause he couldn't breathe right. Had to hook him up to ox'gen. I reckon he'll be all right. Old Doc Shoat said Ben had one of the worst reactions he'd ever seen. Said it's a good thing we got there when we did. Said a few more stings coulda killed him. Said Ben coulda died 'cause he was breaking out and swelling inside same as on the outside. 'Em stings musta hurt like hell."

I winced, remembering how much a single bee sting could hurt. Multiple stings would cause unbearable pain. My heart ached for Ben.

Trickem paused long enough to light a cigarette, take a puff, and blow gray smoke out of the side of his mouth before continuing. I moved a few steps away to avoid the stinking odor.

"Your mama and daddy went on the hospital. Said I could go wif 'em, but I told 'em I'd hitch a ride home. Feller in Chatham give me a ride to the MacKenzie post office. I walked the rest of the way home. Got to thinking that somebody ought to see 'bout the 'bacca and help out 'round here. Stopped by Uncle Travis' place and told 'em what happened. Told 'em I was coming over here. J.R. said he wanted to come, too. Glad he did." Trickem cupped his hand to the side of his mouth and whispered, "I ain't much good at milking cows myself."

Surprised by Trickem's confession, I laughed out loud.

Ole Betsy ambled out of the stable, followed by J.R. with a bucket of warm milk, which he handed to me. I can't remember the last time that I was so grateful to anyone, but I couldn't think of anything to say besides, "Thanks."

"Glad to do it. Now what else needs to be done?" he asked as he reached for the pitchfork to muck the stall.

I went over a list of daily chores that he and Trickem divided between the two of them before I headed to the house with the milk. There I strained the milk several times through a small wire mesh strainer the way mama always did, before pouring it into a clean gallon jar for storage. I wrote the date on a strip of paper that I taped to the jar before making room for it in the refrigerator. While I was straining the milk, I told Eva about the neighbors who had shown up out of the blue to help me.

"Thank you, Lord," she said looking up toward the ceiling. "I didn't know anything else to do, so I asked God to send us some help."

"Well, He sure answered that prayer in a hurry," I said as I washed, dried, and stored the bucket, strainer, and other items that were now cluttering the kitchen sink.

Eva had started a fire in the wood stove and was baking something that smelled delicious, a combination of warm, ripe berries and sweet bread.

"Berry cobbler?" I asked after sniffing the air a few times. "I love blackberry cobbler."

"So do I," Eva said, giving me a warm smile that seemed to light up her creamy complexion with a rosy glow. "I found a bowl of fresh berries in the refrigerator that needed to be cooked. You know they don't keep but a day or two, so I thought I should go ahead and make something—use them up before they go bad." She opened the oven door, allowing the aroma to fill the room, before deciding that the cobbler needed to bake several minutes longer.

"We'll have supper as soon as it's done."

From years of habit, I set the table for four people and poured four glasses of sweet tea while Eva sliced tomatoes, emptied fresh green beans into a bowl, and got the macaroni and cheese casserole from the warming closet over the top of the cook stove.

"Were you expecting company?" Eva asked, noticing the extra places that I'd set.

"No, I guess I wasn't thinking." I paused before saying; "Maybe we could ask J.R. and Trickem to stay for supper, since they were so good about coming to help with the chores."

Her face seemed to harden, furrows creasing between her eyebrows, as she looked at me, apparently stunned that I would suggest such a thing. "No, absolutely not."

"But…but why not?"

"Now, Darla Mae, you know the Bible says that the races ought not to mix. I know your mama and daddy wouldn't want a nigger boy sitting down to their table. They wouldn't even want that lowlife Trickem to eat here. I'm surprised that you would suggest such a thing."

I felt embarrassed and miserable knowing that I had garnered disapproval from someone I liked so much. Eva was such a loving person, yet she had used the "n" word, and obviously thought the people who had come to help us were inferior to us, even though they were capable of doing things that neither of us could do. This kind of thinking didn't make sense to me.

Eva said she had prayed for God to send us some help, was thankful for them, yet she didn't want to show them any earthly appreciation. How could that be? Didn't Jesus cross the street specifically to help the Samaritan? Why, Trickem had probably saved Ben's life by picking those yellow jackets off of him with his bare hands. Weren't we supposed to forgive people for their past transgressions? When we don't forgive, aren't we creating a kind of hell right here on earth? I wanted to argue with Eva that we were all God's children, regardless of the color of our skin, that we are commanded to love our neighbor as ourselves. Since she was an adult, a preacher's wife at that, I thought I ought not to get into an argument with her. At least not that night.

I knew my parents held beliefs that were different from Eva's. They were more tolerant and accepting of people who were different from them. When someone did something nice for them, they immediately found a way to show their appreciation. Finally I thought of something to say, a solution of sorts. "Mama would at least offer them a plate of food that they could eat out on the picnic table."

"No. When your daddy gets home, he can pay these boys for their work. We're *not* going to be feeding them tonight." The finality of her words told me to drop the subject, but I made up my mind right then and there that when I was grown, living on my own, I would have friends of all races. I'd invite these friends to my home where we could share meals together at the same table, side by side.

I was still stewing in my own thoughts when Bug's fussiness demanded my attention. He needed a clean diaper, a bottle of warm milk, a bowl of cereal, and a lot of sisterly cuddling, which I gave him before settling down for my own supper with Eva. She asked me to say the blessing.

"Dear God, I don't know how to thank You enough that Ben is alive. I hope You'll make him well again. Thank You for mama and daddy and Bug and Cousin Charley and Eva. Thank You for Mrs. Russell and J.R. and Trickem and all our other family and friends. Thank You for the food we are about to eat. Bless all the hands that prepared it and all those who are not here to share it. Amen."

In spite of our earlier exchange, Eva and I chatted pleasantly about nothing in particular throughout the meal. News and weather reports from Channel 7 television in Roanoke, VA, provided background noise, as it usually did for evening meals at our house. On the farm we planned our daily activities around these weather reports. "Hazy, hot, and humid," the dreaded three H's continued to be the forecast for this week. That meant more tobacco ripening in the fields to be harvested and more vegetables withering on the vines in the garden. More stuff to pick, shell, can, pickle, or freeze.

"I'll be so glad when September rolls around, when I can start a new school year," I said between bites of blackberry cobbler that was probably staining my teeth and tongue purple. "I love school."

"Oh yeah? What do you love about it?" Eva asked. She had to know the answer because we'd talked about school many times over the past six years.

I pretended to give the question some serious thought before answering. "New teacher, new books, lots of books, more to learn, more time to spend with friends. With all the medical expenses for Ben, I might not get any new clothes. Still, I can hardly wait." I was also thinking that I could hardly wait to get away from all the work on the farm, but I didn't say it.

She chuckled at my answer, rose from the table, and went to the back door to see who had just rattled the screen. Trickem handed her a basket of eggs he had gathered. J.R. told her he'd be back in the morning to do the milking. Trickem said he'd be back, too, and that he and J.R. were going to round up some more help to prime tobacco. Walt had told him he needed to get another curing in the barn before the leaves burned up on the plants. Eva thanked both of them. "I know Walt and Alene will appreciate all y'all are doing to help them out." I went to the door to add my thanks, but they had already started to walk briskly down the road toward their own little farms, their silhouettes disappearing into the setting sun.

Darkness fell amid the sounds of crickets chirping, dogs barking, and an occasional woodpecker hammering away at an old hickory tree in the woods nearby. Fireflies signaled their presence on this hot summer night. Other insects crashed into the window screens, seeking the light of the ceiling fixtures.

Upstairs in my room, I prepared for bed, but decided that I really wanted to be downstairs where the air was cooler. If I slept on the sofa in the living room, I could hear Bug when he woke up during the night. Since Eva was sleeping on the day bed in our living room (the closest thing we had to a guest bed), I'd be close to her, too.

With my pillow, a blanket, and my diary in hand, I joined her in the living room. She'd changed into a pair of mama's best cotton pajamas that I'd given her. They didn't quite fit, but I thought they'd be more comfortable than trying to sleep in a skirt and blouse.

"I thought you'd be asleep already," Eva said. She was propped up against one end of the daybed with mama's Bible open in her hands.

"No, it's too hot upstairs. Mama sometimes lets Ben and me sleep down here when it's really hot or if there's a thunderstorm. Tonight I just wanted to be closer to Bug."

"It is still hot. Little Bug was sweating just lying there in his crib. I bathed and changed him while you were upstairs. He is such a good baby."

"He is such a lucky baby, having so many people to take care of him. He'll be spoiled rotten before he's a year old," I repeated what I'd heard my parents' friends say to mama.

"Could be," she said and went back to her Bible reading.

I spread my blanket over the seat and back of our modern-style sofa and sat down to write for a while in my new diary. As soon as this sofa was delivered, mama had covered it with clear plastic to keep us from messing it up. Daddy complained all the time about the plastic being hot and sticky against a person's body, and so did Ben and I. But mama told us that this was the first nice piece of furniture she'd ever owned and she planned to take good care if it. She said she thought it might have to last her a lifetime, that she'd take the plastic off it when all the kids were grown and gone. Now here I sat, wishing my life away, wishing for the day when I could sit my bottom directly on the bumpy blue upholstery. I might even accidentally (on purpose) spill something on it. Would God forgive me for such a mean thought?

Sleep came quickly, probably because I was exhausted, physically and emotionally, from everything that had happened. Before I dozed, I said a silent prayer that Ben would be all right and that my parents would be home the next day. I also asked God to help me to be a better person, one who wouldn't do mean things just to hurt other people.

"Hell's only half full," a seductive masculine voice said. "Come join us. Come see what delightful experiences we have to offer." The voice was coming from a pit of blue-white flames. I

157

was being drawn toward that pit, toward those flames, like a moth drawn toward the bare light bulb on the back porch. Dancing figures whirled to fast-paced music, their bodies bumping and grinding against one another. Other figures laughed in a jovial manner. I wanted to dance with them, laugh with them, and share their secrets. But when I started to move in their direction, a gigantic white-gloved hand stopped me. It grabbed my wrist and pulled me after it, taking me into a tunnel that grew more and more narrow. My whole body was being squeezed smaller and smaller. I couldn't breathe. I was suffocating in there. "Let me go! Let me go!" I screamed, and kicked again and again as I tried to free myself.

"Darla Mae, Darla Mae," a female voice was softly calling my name. "Darla Mae, are you OK?" the woman asked as she gently lifted my head off the pillow. Before I could answer, she continued in a firm, reassuring voice, "You *are* OK. I'm here with you." The voice belonged to Eva.

I shook my head a few times to clear away the last images of the nightmare, opened my eyes, and looked into her worried ones.

"I'm so glad…" I said before I started to sob. Eva quickly brought me a handkerchief and a glass of water. My screams had awakened Bug, so she brought him into the living room where she sat rocking him until he went back to sleep.

"Do you want to tell me about the dream?" she asked calmly. Something in her voice and manner inspired confidence. I thought she must have had plenty of experience with people having nightmares.

For several minutes, I sat there debating with myself about whether or not I wanted to tell her about my recurring dreams. On the one hand, I really needed to talk to somebody. If I told Eva, she might be able to help me figure out a way to make them stop. On the other hand, she might tell my parents, who would think I was going crazy. There was no telling what they might do. They might try to send me off to that hospital in Stanton where they keep crazy people.

"Darla Mae," Eva called my name again. "It's OK to talk about your dreams. Everybody has dreams. Sometimes they're frightening dreams. If you talk about them, they might stop."

Her words were encouraging enough that I decided to tell her about the nightmares that I'd been having off and on over the past two years. I described them in all the vivid detail I could remember. She listened but didn't say anything until I had finished.

"No wonder you were kicking and screaming." Her voice seemed to be filled with compassion. "What do you think would make you dream something like that?" she asked.

"I don't know," I said. Immediately, I hated myself for lying to this sweet lady who was trying to help me.

"Yes, I do know," I confessed. "I'm afraid I'll go to hell."

"Darla Mae!" Her voice registered the shock that I had anticipated. "What on earth would make you think such a thing?"

"Preachers," I said, trying to read her reaction in the dim lamplight. "Well, not Cousin Charley so much as Reverend Hardshell at Healing Waters. He's always telling the congregation that they're a bunch of sorry sinners. That they'll burn in hell forever if they don't repent immediately."

"But they're talking about adults who do bad things," Eva interrupted me.

"No. Reverend Hardshell looks right at *me* when he says the part about burning. I can almost see the fires of hell glowing in his eyes. It's a scary sight. And he's not the only one. Sister Sarah hounded me at your church Sunday night."

"Sister Sarah?"

"Yeah. She called me a 'little goody two-shoes' who would do plenty of things that are wrong. She even said I'd burn in hell if I didn't get my life right with God before I turn twelve."

Eva glanced at the ceiling while giving her head a negative shake. She kept her lips tightly clenched as if she was trying not to say what she was thinking.

I paused a moment, remembering the encounter. "I'm afraid that I can't be a good little Christian girl for my whole life. I've already broken three commandments that I know about and maybe some others. But I'm not even sure what some of them mean. Like the one about not committing adultery." I looked up at her, hoping to have her explain that one to me, but she was trying to get Bug into a more comfortable position on her lap.

"I know I'll mess up somewhere along the way. That's why I haven't joined a church yet. Daddy says joining a church requires *serious* commitment." There, I'd said it, confessed my weaknesses. A warm sense of relief swept over me, immediately followed by a strong sense of what

Mrs. Rivers called "vulnerability." I'd left myself open to lectures, criticism, suspicion, and who knew what else.

Eva cradled my sleeping baby brother in her arms. Her soft blue eyes seemed to search the wall behind me for clues that might lead her to a proper response. I thought she might be wrestling with herself about whether to convey official church doctrine or some interpretation of her own.

"Serious commitment, Darla Mae, starts with loving the Lord with all your heart and all your soul and all your mind. Do you truly love God?"

"That's hard for me to say. Certainly not like I love mama, daddy, Ben, and Bug. I can see them and talk with them and touch them. It's harder to love someone you never get to see. As for loving with all my soul—I haven't figured out where that's located. And my mind, oh my… my mind just wanders around all over the place. Even when I'm in church trying to pay attention, it is often on school or friends or the latest rock 'n' roll song. On Sunday I saw some cardinals outside the church window and got to thinking how I'd like to fly away with them." I paused for a moment before I asked, "How can anybody, including Sister Sarah, say they love God with all their heart, soul, and mind?"

"That's a very good question." Eva's chair creaked against the linoleum rug, as she rocked back and forth. She seemed to be carefully weighing my words. I liked the fact that she wasn't condemning me, nor was she trying to influence my beliefs, the way I thought a preacher's wife might.

"You also need to ask yourself if you repent of your sins, although I can't imagine that you have any sins to be concerned about," Eva said finally.

I squirmed around on the sofa, sat upright, and folded my legs Indian style before I confessed. "I stole an apple when I was seven years old. Mama made me take it back to the store and apologize to Mrs. Russell. I haven't stolen anything since, but not long ago I used the Lord's name in vain. Mama beat the tar out of me." As easy as it was for me to tell her all this, I still didn't want to talk about the secrets I was keeping about mama. Instead, I said "On top of that, I am not always completely honest, especially when I know I am in trouble with mama about something."

Eva chuckled, apparently finding my misdeeds a bit amusing. After a few minutes, she spoke again. "Serious commitment also has to do with your presence, your prayers, your gifts, and your service to God. Do you have any problem with any of those areas?"

I thought about this for several moments. "Well, presence could be a problem since we don't go to church every Sunday and we never go on Wednesday nights for prayer meetings."

Eva nodded her head in agreement.

"Prayer is no problem, since I pray every day, sometimes several times a day. I even pray in school, silent prayers before most tests, especially pop quizzes."

Eva grinned, shifting Bug into a more comfortable position in her arms. He made little soft snoring noises, drew himself into a fetal position, and sucked on his thumb.

"Gifts are a problem. Ten percent of nothing is still nothing, until I can earn some money someday. I did put 10% of what I earned picking hornworms off the tobacco plants this week into the collection plate, but that was almost nothing. Service is not a problem, so long as I can get to wherever something is being done. I like doing things to help other people. It seems like the right thing to do and it makes me happy. I don't have a problem with any of that. What I have a problem with is being good."

"Being good?" Eva's eyebrows scrunched together, creating a wrinkle over her pug nose and little lines radiating out from the corners of her eyes.

"Yeah, sometimes I want to be bad, really bad. But I don't want to go to hell."

Eva chuckled again. "I don't suppose anybody does! But what do you mean by being bad?"

"Well, sometimes it's little things. Earlier this evening I was thinking about how I'd like to spill something on this sofa, just to get even with mama for keeping it covered up with this stupid plastic for so many years."

Eva's smirk told me that she might enjoy doing the same thing.

"Other times, it's more significant stuff I want to do. Reverend Hardshell is always condemning people who drink and dance and fornicate. Well, I think dancing feels good and I want to keep right on dancing." I told her this in complete sincerity but realized that I could get myself into big trouble by telling such things to a preacher's wife. "You won't tell my parents about any of this, will you?" I swallowed hard and waited for her to respond. She shook her head sideways, still holding onto a thin-lipped smile.

"I haven't yet had anything to drink that would make me intoxicated, but from what I've seen of people who do drink, it doesn't look like such a bad thing. Seems like to me those people are having a really good time. So, is it wrong to have fun?" I took a deep breath before I could even say the next thing on my mind. "And fornicating— well, I don't even know what that word means, but I think it must be more fun than drinking and dancing. Otherwise, why would Reverend Hardshell condemn it so passion-ately? I know I want to try it someday."

Eva's right hand went over her mouth, but I could see the corners of her lips climbing up the side of her face. The merriment in her eyes told me I had said something she found amusing, but I didn't know what it was.

"Well," she finally said. "Well, hum…" She giggled. For the second time today, Eva seemed to be at a loss for words. She leaned forward, planted both feet firmly on the floor, and gently lifted Bug as she stood. "I'll put Bug back in his crib. Then you and I need to get some sleep. Maybe we can talk some more tomorrow."

"Maybe," I said, hoping that Eva could enlighten me, especially about the meaning of *that* word. There were other ideas that I was having trouble reconciling with church beliefs—concepts about racial differences, hypocrisy, forgiveness, and such. There was also the mat-ter of what I had heard my mama say and what I had seen her doing. Would I ever be able to tell anyone about those incidents?

The mantel clock chimed the hour—two a.m. I plumped up my pillow, closed my eyes, and tried to close my mind to the ugly possibility that there were questions that might never be answered to my satisfaction. There were situations in which I had no control. Not now. Maybe not ever.

Chapter 19

I was sweeping the last of the yesterday's grass and grit off the back porch when I saw a highly-polished new Buick roll to a stop in our driveway. It bore a New York license plate. I didn't know anybody in New York. In fact, I didn't know anybody who lived any farther away than North Carolina, unless you counted the cousins in California who sent us Christmas cards every year; but I'd never seen any of them. If those people from New York had been from another galaxy, they wouldn't have generated any more excitement for me. I loved meeting folks from "foreign places."

My excitement was tempered when I saw Aunt Essie emerge from the passenger side of the car, wearing a gray gingham housedress that draped softly around her ample figure. She was carrying a huge platter of something covered with aluminum foil. The aroma of fried chicken had my mouth watering before I could even say hello.

Latisha, who had gotten out of the back seat, sauntered toward me carrying a pie-shaped container. Her red plaid shirt and denim pedal pushers showed slight curves in her chest and butt. Just a day or so ago, mama had said Latisha was too young to be "maturing" like that.

Dead grass crunched under my bare feet as I ran to meet them. "Hey," I yelled.

Eva had seen the car and came quickly behind me, carrying Bug on her right hip. She stopped a few feet away from Aunt Essie and stood there, arms wrapped around the baby. Bug began reaching for me, making little whining noises that told me he wanted the comfort of a familiar person's touch. I took him from Eva and began to blow lightly on the thin hair on his head while whispering, "The wind goes woo-woo." He giggled and shrieked before putting his hand in my mouth. I jostled him on my hip as I went to greet our visitors.

"Hey, Darla Mae, how y'all doing?" Aunt Essie looked at me, her haggard face a mass of brown wrinkles, more pronounced than ever after her week of grieving. Coarse black hair peeked from beneath a blue print kerchief.

"We're doing OK, Aunt Essie," I said, wanting to be positive but not too cheerful.

"And little Ben? J.R. said he got stung real bad by a swarm of yellow jackets."

I had to take Bug's fingers out of my mouth again before I could answer. "Ben's probably going to be OK. He might even get to come home today."

"Well, I'm glad to hear it!" I saw a hint of a smile play on her thick lips.

"We brought you a chocolate buttermilk pie." Latisha held out the container she was carrying. "I made it myself." Her eyes twinkled with a mischievous look that told me she was probably lying. Aunt Essie's sideways glance confirmed my suspicions.

"Do I have to share it with anybody?" I asked, knowing full well I did. This time I was the one being scolded by Aunt Essie's brown-eyed gaze.

"Yes, you do," Eva said, from behind me, her arms crossed over her chest.

I motioned for her to move forward. "Come meet our friends. This is Aunt Essie, J.R.'s grandmother, and this is his sister, Latisha."

Then I turned to Eva and introduced her as the wife of my father's first cousin, Reverend Charley Hill. "She's an extra special cousin. Seems like some of my favorite kin folks are the ones I'm not even related to," I added, smiling up at her.

After Eva and Aunt Essie exchanged the usual polite responses, Aunt Essie offered the platter she was carrying to Eva. "J.R. said him an' some more were gonna prime 'bacco over here today. I knew Miss Alene wasn't here to do any cooking for the help, so I had my oldest daughter, Imogene—that's her there in the car—I had her to fry some chicken this morning. We been eatin' chicken for the past week now. Lawd, I don't believe you could pay me to eat any mo' chicken any time soon." She chuckled, a faint-hearted attempt at laughter.

"Thank you. That's so thoughtful of you," Eva said, "especially at a time when you are dealing with your own loss. I was sorry to hear about your husband. Darla Mae told me how everybody around here thought highly of him."

I saw Aunt Essie struggle to hold back her tears. "He was a good man. Him and Mr. Walter had a real special friendship. They used to spend evenings together picking out tunes on 'ey guitars. Good men. Both of 'em." She took a deep breath and let it out slowly. "I guess we best be gettin' on back home. Latisha, she gonna stay and help with the 'bacco or whatever else y'all might need her to do." She squinted against the bright sunlight. "Now, 'Tisha, you and Miss Darla Mae behave yo'selves."

"Awe, we will grandma. You know we *always* be good." Latisha blushed right through her pretty coffee cream complexion.

Back inside the house, we stored the chicken in the warming closet above the wood stove, put the pie in the refrigerator, and discussed our plans for the midday meal, when we would feed ourselves plus five hungry workers. Eva concluded that we had plenty of everything, except for some fresh corn, which Latisha and I volunteered to gather from the south garden while Eva made mashed potatoes, biscuits, and gravy.

I put Bug in his playpen in the living room where he could roll around to his little heart's content without anyone having to worry about him. He grabbed his teething ring with both hands and guided it into his mouth where he chomped on it with toothless gums. Pulling it out, he waved the soft rubber ring in front of his nose before tasting it again.

Latisha and I chattered away while we picked corn from stalks that had started to dry in the August heat. We brushed aside blades of corn stalks that scratched our arms in order to reach the succulent young ears that would be boiled, then coated with butter and salt. I got hungry just thinking about how good they were going to taste.

"Old Ben is going to be sorry he's not here to eat his fill of corn on the cob," Latisha said, adding a few more ears to our basket. "You reckon he'll get home today?"

"I sure hope so." I told her about how I'd missed him and my parents the night before. Then I decided to tell her about last night's dream.

"You still havin' 'em nightmares about goin' to hell?" Latisha stared at me. "Girl, what is wrong with you?"

"Nothing is wrong with me. I don't know why I dream what I dream. I just do. Why does anybody dream what they dream?" I stopped picking corn, looked her in the eye, and waited for some enlightenment from my friend.

"I think folks dream what they do 'cause of something they trying to work out in they minds. You been trying to decide what to do about getting saved. If you ax me, I'd tell you to just walk on down the aisle at one of 'em churches you go to. Cry a little bit. Make folks happy for you. Get yo'self dunked here in Holy Pond and be done with it. That's what I did. Ain't no big thing. I don't know what you so worried about. What you think it could be?"

"Well, it's like I told Eva last night. I'm afraid that I'll go to hell because I haven't been saved. But I don't think I can be good all my life."

"You, Darla Mae? You've always been such a *nice* girl. What do you mean, you can't be good?" Her voice was teasing, the way it always was with me.

"You know. Dancing, drinking, and all that adultery stuff. And I'm all mixed up about what is right and wrong, since it seems to me that the Bible tells us to obey God's commandments, yet some people in the church don't, or at least it seems to me that they don't. Sure wish I could figure everything out so that I can get some sleep. If I have to have dreams, I'd rather dream about the day I finish school."

Latisha interrupted me to say, "Uh-huh. And?"

"Earn my own money."

"Uh-huh. And?" Latisha held up two fingers, counting off the litany that had become a familiar refrain in our conversations.

"Have a life of my own." I pronounced this one with considerable conviction.

"Uh-huh. That's three. And?"

"And indoor plumbing," I completed my list and picked up the basket that was now filled with corn.

Latisha laughed the way she always did when I ceased to be serious.

"You left out one," she said, her intelligent eyes dancing, "the day you find out what fornicating means."

"When I find out, I'll probably be dreaming about it, too." I smiled at her, a wide toothy grin that she imitated. "Let's get this stuff back to the house. It won't be long before we'll have some hungry workers here wanting a good meal," I said, walking away from the garden.

"Yeah, like you and me." Latisha reminded me.

We continued to chat about this and that, but in the back of my mind I was wondering what Eva would do about eating arrangements. The workers, black and white, would eat at two picnic tables in the back yard. That was no problem, but what about Latisha? After what Eva had said last night, I knew that having her at the table with us was out of the question, unless I could think of something quick.

When the meal was almost ready, Latisha walked to the tobacco fields to tell everyone that midday dinner was about to be served. I sat our table in the kitchen for three.

"Mama always lets Latisha eat with me," I told Eva.

It was a lie, of course, but close to the truth in that mama would let her sit at the counter while all our family ate at the kitchen table. Eva seemed too preoccupied with getting all the food in separate dishes to notice. I said a silent prayer that my parents wouldn't get home in time to ruin my plan.

Latisha returned with J.R., Trickem, and the other workers, whose shirts were filthy with wet sweat rings and tobacco tar. All of them stopped at the outside spigot where we had aluminum wash pans, some homemade lye soap, and old washcloths available for cleaning up. The men splashed cold water on their faces, arms, and hands before they vigorously scrubbed off a half-day's accumulation of grime. J.R. picked up a wash pan and poured cold water over the top of his head, letting it run down over his shirt and pants. Judging from his pleasant groan and gentle sway, I knew that must have felt good.

I took beverage orders—sweet iced tea or iced water—while Latisha poured them. Together we took the bowls of food and drinks to the picnic tables where we made sure that there was one bowl of each item on each table. Steam rose from the hot food, filling the air with the enticing aromas of fresh-baked biscuits, fried chicken, and assorted vegetables.

J.R. surveyed the table, rubbed his abdomen, and announced, "I can't wait. My stomach has been rubbing my backbone for at least an hour."

"Mine, too," said Trickem. "I could eat this whole platter of chicken by myself."

The other men who had been at work for about five hours, long enough after breakfast to be really hungry again, told him they'd fight him for it. They proceeded to take their seats at wooden picnic tables that daddy had cobbled together long ago. Without anybody saying anything about the seating arrangements, J.R. and two colored men took their places at one table while Trickem and one white fellow sat at the other one.

While we were out there in the shade of those old oak trees I whispered to Latisha, "You are going to eat at the table with us today. Just act like you always do that."

Her hazel eyes sparkled. She grinned, a wide grin that showed off perfectly-aligned front teeth. "Darla Mae, you is right about being bad. If yo mama an' 'em come home while I be eatin' at 'yo table, all hell likely to break loose."

"Just act normal, like we eat together all the time," I whispered again. Latisha nodded her head in agreement as we went through the back door.

Inside I took my usual place at the table and pointed to Ben's usual spot for Latisha. She gave me a slightly worried look before taking her seat.

Eva joined us, sitting in mama's usual place. Her eyes were darting back and forth between Latisha and me.

Finally she glared at me the way daddy does when I am doing something that he doesn't like. Eva seemed uncertain what she wanted to say, sitting there with her thin lips pursed, arms crossed over her bust. "Well… Well, I've never…,"she muttered before she asked, "Who wants to say grace?"

I volunteered and said a quick little prayer out loud. While my eyes were still closed I silently asked God to keep my folks away until this "historic" meal was over. We served ourselves from the bowl nearest us, then passed bowls left and right until all three of us had some of everything—chicken, green beans, mashed potatoes, gravy, sliced tomatoes, corn on the cob, butterbeans, and biscuits.

"Eva, you made biscuits from scratch," I said, as I took one from a napkin-covered plate.

"I tried to make some. They're not as good as your mama's, though."

"Well, Mrs. Hill, I think they're perfect," Latisha said, as she held one up to admire it.

"Oh, they're not perfect, but thank you for saying so." Eva glanced sideways toward Latisha.

We ate in silence for several minutes, intent on devouring our food with as little interruption as possible. I noticed that Latisha sat up straight and ate with her left hand in her lap. She was even cutting chicken off the bone, one bite at a time.

When Eva finally broke the silence by asking Latisha what grade she was in at school, Latisha answered, "In September, I'll be in the seventh grade, the same as Darla Mae."

"Uh-huh. And where is your school?"

"I go to Langston. It is all the way over on the other side of Chatham."

"Goodness. That is a long bus ride." Eva grimaced and then took a bite from the chicken drumstick that she was holding.

I hoped Eva had not noticed that I was staring at Latisha. In the four years I had known her, I had never heard her speak with such perfect grammar. She could have been one of the teachers at my school.

"Yes, ma'am, it is a long ride. But it is worth it to be able to get a good education. The walk is the worst part. We have to walk all the way to Reynolds's Store to catch the bus. That's about three miles from our farm."

Eva stared at Latisha. "Are you telling me that you have to walk three miles just to catch the bus and another three miles to get back home again in the evening? Why can't the bus stop out here on the road next to your farm?"

"I don't mean any disrespect, ma'am, but I think you can look at me and understand why I have to go to the school where I do and how I do." Latisha stirred butterbeans with her fork and looked up at me with guarded eyes. I knew this school business was a sensitive subject with her.

Eva swallowed hard and shook her head left to right. "Well, it just doesn't seem right. The county ought to build a school for you out here in MacKenzie and stop the bus in front of your farm, the same as they do for Ben and Darla Mae." I saw her eyes spin as if she suddenly realized what her statement had implied.

"Yes, ma'am, that would be really nice. Really convenient, too. I don't expect that will happen any time soon, but one day I hope that other colored children will be able to go to a new school where they will have new books, new equipment, and more opportunities than I have had." Latisha stared at her plate and then looked up at me as if asking for help.

"If our world was perfect, we'd be going to the same school on the same bus, getting the same education." I blurted out the thought that had been hanging in the back of my mind for a long time. Now Eva knew where I stood, which might cause her to like me less, but that was a chance I felt I had to take.

"Darla Mae, you seem to want all things in your world to be fair and equal." Eva's stare held my eyes to hers, searing her words into my memory. "As you get older you will find that there are lots of ways in which life seems unfair. Sometimes you can do something about it, sometimes you can't. You just have to trust God to help you figure out the best way to make things better."

As if on cue, Bug started bawling at the top of his little lungs. I jumped up, ran to his crib, and picked him up. He continued to blubber for a couple of minutes, but settled down after I changed him and brought him to the table where I fed him tiny bits of gravy covered bread and some mashed up beans. As soon as his bottle was ready, I held him in my left arm and allowed him to suck it down in noisy gulps.

Eva and Latisha continued to talk while I took care of Bug, but I wasn't tuned into their conversation. The fact that they were talking seemed significant to me. If this communication changed the way Eva viewed colored people, then my little white lie might have been worthwhile.

⁂

After Latisha and I cleared the tables, stored the food, and washed the dishes, we walked slowly to the tobacco barn where we would help with handing and stringing the leaves. Eva said that she'd stay at the house and play with Bug for a while before she joined us. I told her not to worry about coming to the barn since we could provide all the extra help that would be needed there that day.

Normally I would have preferred to stay with Bug. Being clean, being under the shade of a big oak tree, and being able to sit down was certainly more appealing than an afternoon spent moving sticky ole tobacco leaves from the slides to the bench, making bunches of them, and stringing them. That was hot, hard, nasty work, but today I didn't mind it so much because Latisha was helping.

As soon as we were out of Eva's earshot, I grabbed Latisha by the arm and asked, "What was that all about at dinner today?"

"What you mean?" She stopped, removed my hand from her arm, and squinted her eyes to block the white-hot sun overhead.

"I mean—I have never heard you speak with such perfect grammar before. You sounded like a white girl. Why don't you talk like that all the time?"

Latisha laughed. The more she laughed, the louder she laughed. She doubled over, held her sides, and danced around while I stood there not having a clue.

"What's so funny?" I asked.

"I was acting," Latisha said finally.

"Acting?" I still didn't see why that was so funny.

"Yeah. I was pretending that I was someone special who had come to dinner at the white family's house. In order to make a good impression, I needed to be on my best behavior. Judging from Mrs. Hill's reaction, my performance was convincing."

"Acting, huh? Who taught you to act like that?" It occurred to me that there might be a lot that I didn't know about my friend.

"My mama. She was an actress in New York. My mama was right. She say—no, she *said*—that if I ever want to get ahead in this world, I need to learn to speak the white man's English language correctly. When I lived with her, she never let me use what she called 'trash talk.' I just started talking like colored folks around here when J.R. and I came to live with grandma. The kids at my school made fun of me. They called me an 'uppity nigga,' so I started using their expressions in order to fit in. After a while, it just felt natural." I saw Latisha's shoulders slump ever so slightly. "Mama also said I needed to learn to use good manners, the manners of upper-class white folks." She pretended to blot her lips with a napkin.

"You mean the ones who cut their chicken off the bone instead of eating it with their fingers?" I asked.

"Yeah. Yes. She used to work for a doctor and his wife, preparing food and serving their company meals, before she got her break in acting. The doctor's wife sent mama to school and spent time at home teaching her about all sorts of things that poor people, especially poor colored people, never know. Shucks, we didn't even own salad forks, oyster forks, and butter knives. How were we supposed to know when to use them?"

I wanted to ask her what an oyster fork was, but there were more important questions that had to be answered first. "What's your mama's name? Has she made any movies?" I was definitely shocked to know that my friend's mother might be somebody famous. "Why haven't you told me about your mother in all the years I've known you?"

A slight smile played on her thick lips. "Mama was Clarissa Cordoe. That was her stage name. Mostly she acted in off-Broadway theaters where there was a part for a black female and no white person was available or willing to paint herself for it."

"Where is she now? Why aren't you living with her?" Curiosity got the best of my manners, but I immediately regretted my inquisitiveness when I saw Latisha's uniquely angular face transition from happy to sad. Tears formed and slid slowly down her face.

I hugged her and said, "I'm sorry. I didn't mean to upset you."

She sniffled before flicking away tears with her right hand. "Mama in a special hospital where she gonna be for the rest of her life," Latisha whimpered, making a whipped puppy sound.

"Oh, Latisha, I'm so sorry. What happened?" A split second later I added, "If you don't want to talk about it, that's OK." A part of me wanted to know, but I didn't want to cause Latisha any more pain.

Latisha stopped to lean against the trunk of an old oak tree. She collected herself and started to speak. "Mama was eager to make acting her career so she wouldn't have to be cookin' and cleanin' for anybody ever again. She do about anything to get ahead. She left my daddy and got involved wid dis man who claim he can make her a star. He started giving her some stuff that he say gonna expand her mind. Guess that what happen, if you can call a stroke a way to expand yo mind. When he find her, she almost dead. Might as well have been. She don't know she in the world now. Just lay in her bed and stare at the walls. Don't know me. Don't know daddy. I can't stand to see her that way." Latisha cried great heaving sobs that shook her slender shoulders.

I didn't know what to say, so I did the only thing I could think of. I searched my pants pocket for a handkerchief to offer her. The one I found was an almost new one that Cousin Charley had handed to me the day before. It had been used on one end, so I tore it in half and gave her the clean end. "Here, you can have this," I said as I handed it to her.

Latisha took the handkerchief half, dried her eyes, and daintily blew her nose.

"Darla Mae, you won't tell anybody about my mama will you? We just don't talk about her anymore. It's as if she died a long time ago, but we haven't been able to bury her yet."

My heart ached for the enormity of Latisha's loss. No matter how mad I might get with my mother at times, no matter how much I hated what she had said and done, I wanted her to be alive and healthy forever. I couldn't imagine life without her. I hugged Latisha again. "You don't have to worry about me telling anybody anything." I thumped my chest and said "I am the world's best keeper of secrets. And if you ever want to talk about her again, I am here to listen." I felt like I was growing up right there on the spot, somehow becoming more mature as we talked. I also knew that I would soon share my secrets with Latisha.

"Thanks," Latisha whispered. She started walking toward the tobacco barn. I fell in step with her and soon we made a pact to practice our schoolhouse English on each other. She also agreed to teach me some society manners, which we both agreed that we might need when we grew up.

"And you know what else, Latisha?" I asked, eager to let her know what was in my heart. "Someday you and I are going to go up to Washington, DC, to talk with the president of the United States about how he ought to make it possible for all children, regardless of the color of their skin, to go to school together, to ride the bus together, to eat in restaurants together, and whatever else it is that they want to do."

"Darla Mae, you sure got some big dreams. Going up to the White House, talking to the president." Latisha thought for a moment, flashed me a grin of pure delight and said "Let's do it."

"Yes, let's do it," I said, knowing that this was one serious commitment I wanted to keep. Before long we were back to laughing and cutting up with each other the way we always did. We had just become better friends than ever.

Ben, mama, daddy, and Cousin Charley arrived late that afternoon while Latisha and I were at the barn, helping to string tobacco leaves onto sticks that would later be hung up there. One of them, probably Cousin Charley, honked the horn to alert us to their return. I dropped the bunch of leaves in my hand and ran to the house as fast as I could. Mama went inside before I got to them.

"Ben, wait! Ben!" I ran to his side to give him a hug, something I was not accustomed to doing. He saw what I was about to do and took a step backward away from me, instead giving me a pretend punch in the left shoulder. Same old Ben, I thought. I gave him a big, cheesy grin that said, "I love you too, big brother." Then I gently punched him in the shoulder for real.

"Yeah, I'm home. Back to my old self. Thanks to Trickem. That crazy man picked those yellow jackets off me with his bare hands." Ben's tanned face lit up like a light bulb as he continued his story. "And daddy. Daddy drove like a maniac. And old Dr. Shoat's eyes got so big I thought they were going to pop right out of his head. Even though I could barely see when we got there, I could see his eyes— the way they were magnified by his glasses. He gave me a shot with a twenty-penny nail. It felt like it was that big anyway." Ben held up both hands about a foot apart to illustrate the size of the needle. "Then I was hauled off to the hospital with the sirens screaming, where the doctors and nurses poked and punched more holes in me." He pointed to a piece of gauze taped over his arm. "They put some contraption over my nose so I could breathe better and wrapped a bandage around my sprained ankle. Today they X-rayed my ankle and ran some tests to be sure that I was OK to go home. So, I'm sorry, sis, but I'm going to hang around here to harass your skinny butt for a few more years." Any other time his taunting words would have irritated me, but that day I was genuinely pleased that my beloved brother was alive and well enough to annoy me.

"Thank God for that," I said. Cousin Charley, who'd been quietly exchanging knowing looks with my daddy said, "Amen."

Daddy put his hand on my shoulder, examined the tobacco gum on my arms, and said, "Looks like you've got things under control around here, Darla Mae. Maybe I'll turn the farming over to you." He rumpled my hair and gave me an affectionate hug. I felt simultaneously loved and appreciated, emotions that I hoped daddy could see reflected in my misty eyes.

"I've had plenty of help, thanks to Eva, Trickem, J.R., and Latisha. And Mrs. Russell and Aunt Essie. I don't know what I would have done without them. J.R. and Trickem came last night to help with the chores. Then they came back this morning to do the same thing, only this time they brought some more help. They're in the fields right now, priming tobacco. Trickem said you'd planned to prime it today. There was enough for a curing, so he and J.R. rounded up some other neighbors to help get it in the barn."

Daddy must have been stunned because he said, "Well, I'll be damn!" right in front of Cousin Charley. When he realized what he'd done, he apologized to Charley. "I don't know what to say about people just showing up to help out like this."

"There are a lot of good people in this world. Even Trickem. There's some good in that old boy yet." Cousin Charley observed. "Why, these folks are doing no more than you might have done for one of them in similar circumstances."

"Maybe so." Daddy stood there in the driveway, shaking his head. "I guess I ought to get on down to the bottoms and see what they're doing. Ben, you help at the barn. Sit and hand leaves so that you can keep your ankle elevated. I don't want you in any of the fields until we get rid of whatever yellow jacket nests there might be in them. Charley, you're welcome to help with the tobacco," daddy's steel gray eyes teased Cousin Charley's brown ones, "if you remember how."

Cousin Charley returned daddy's smug grin. "Oh, I think I remember how. In fact, I remember stringing three sticks of tobacco to your one when we were about Ben's age. I probably still can." Cousin Charley said. "I've got some work clothes in the trunk of my car that I keep in there just in case I have to change a tire or do something like that on the way to church. I'll slip them on and join you. It might be fun to work in tobacco again."

"Humh," daddy snorted as he strolled down the path toward the old log barn where some of the weary farm hands were working off their hearty midday dinner.

Chapter 20

Three days had passed since Ben's return from the hospital. In that time, everything had settled into the normal rhythm of farm life. Taking care of the chores, helping mama with the canning, playing with Kati, and babysitting Bug filled my days. I longed for the return to school, where my mind could be stimulated, where new challenges awaited me, and where my friends were always present and into something fun.

When daddy announced at breakfast on Saturday morning that he'd like to have a weenie roast at the tobacco barn that evening, I felt a surge of energy that I always felt when there was a change of pace from our everyday routine. A weenie roast meant we'd have hot dogs, a rare and wonderful treat at our house. Coleslaw, baked beans, brownies, and homemade ice cream would accompany them, along with whatever else mama wanted to put on the table. Her menus usually included whatever we had available in the garden at the time.

"Mama, I'll make the brownies and coleslaw," I quickly volunteered.

"OK, but you be sure to make the coleslaw the way I taught you. Not too much sugar. It's not supposed to be sweet. And make enough to have plenty of extras. You never know who might drop by."

Mama raised Bug above her head and blew loud kisses against his bare belly, causing him to squeal and squirm with delight. I noticed mama's face was radiant, glowing, and reflecting so much love for this child that I couldn't help but be a little bit envious. More than a little envious. Suddenly, I felt an overwhelming need to get out of the house and away from them.

"I'll run out to the garden and get a big cabbage head while the dew is still on it," I said, as I grabbed a knife to use in the task. Out the back door I went, not caring that the screen door slammed shut behind me. I heard mama ask for probably the thousandth time, "Were you raised in a barn?"

I trudged down the well-worn path to the garden where a row of tender green cabbage was developing into large, firm heads. The sun was already high in the sky, starting to dry the dew that had risen overnight, coating the weeds between the rows with moisture that now glistened. It was a sight I loved. Sunlight sparkling like diamonds off these ordinary plants lifted my spirits. I wiggled my bare toes through the weeds and felt the cool wetness that never failed to be invigorating. My thoughts turned to the many ways that God blessed our lives. We might not have much money, but we were very, very rich in ordinary pleasures.

Scents of fresh vegetables, some overly ripe tomatoes, and one decaying cabbage filled the air. I searched for a perfectly round, heavy head of cabbage, which I cut cleanly from its stalk, before searching for the decomposing vegetables, which I removed to the compost pile near the garden. Being alone in the garden always gave me time to think, to reflect, to dream, and to plan. I took my time with the tasks at hand, delaying the moment of my return to mama's constant criticism.

In spite of all the excitement about Ben's return, Eva had told mama about Latisha eating at the table with us. What she actually told mama was that she really liked my colored friend who was so smart and so well-mannered. Mama was furious—not so much about my sharing my eating space with a colored person (something that was strictly forbidden in white society, even poor white society), but she was livid because I had lied to Eva when I told her she let us eat together all the time. That night she made me write a letter to Eva, telling her I had told a lie and asking her to forgive me. Then she made me write "I must not tell a lie" a hundred times, just like the teachers made misbehaving students do in third grade.

"You have to live by the Ten Commandments," she said, "whether you like it or not."

As I removed the tough outer leaves of the cabbage head, I thought about my other conversations with Eva a few days ago. I wondered if she had said anything to mama about my nightmares. If she had, mama had said nothing to me. Not knowing was worse than knowing. I had to be prepared in case mama ever did bring up the subject of the dreams, so I used this time to think about what I would say to her that might be convincing without telling her that she was a big factor in my nightmares.

"Darla Mae!" mama leaned out of the screen door and hollered to me. "You've had plenty of time to cut a head of cabbage. Get on back here. I need your help in the kitchen."

"I'm coming," I yelled back, kicking a clod of dirt out of my way as I walked toward the house. "There is always something that you need my help to do," I muttered to myself before plastering on a smile that more clearly matched the mood I'd been in before mama had interrupted my thinking.

"What took you so long?" mama asked when I came through the door.

"I was adding some stuff to the compost pile," I told her, "stuff that had gone bad."

"Well, I hope you didn't throw away anything that could have been used. You know we can't afford to be throwing away perfectly good food." Mama brushed a strand of hair away from her face to inspect the cabbage that I handed her.

Could I ever do anything right, I wondered. Instead of acknowledging mama's comment, I got a cutting board and grater from the cabinet, a bottle of apple cider vinegar and a quarter cup of sugar from the pantry, and then went to the refrigerator for a jar of mayonnaise. In no time at all, I had washed the cabbage, grated it into finely-chopped pieces, and mixed it with the three basic ingredients of good southern coleslaw.

"I told you not to put too much sugar in it," mama said after tasting it. "Now you need to add some salt and a little more vinegar to cut the sweet."

I complied, making adjustments until the coleslaw met with her approval. Mama and I worked in the kitchen as we often did, without conversation, each of us absorbed in our tasks and our own private thoughts. Our little plastic radio was tuned to WBTM, which was playing country music in the background.

"I go out walking… after midnight, out in the moon-light… searching everywhere…" I started to sing along with a Patsy Cline tune while beating together the ingredients for brownies. Mama's mood changed with the music. She started to sing along, too. We tried to harmonize but ended up laughing at our inability to carry the tune. This moment felt so good, I wanted to find a way to make it last throughout the day.

We sang along with some other tunes, stopping when Bug started to fret. Mama took care of him while I made deviled eggs and the custard base for ice cream that we'd hand-churn later. Today had already been special. I had a feeling it was going to get even better before it was over.

By late afternoon, mama had completed the household chores and taken her bath in preparation for a trip to Russell's store for hot dogs, buns, some rock salt, and a bag of ice. She was wearing a bright yellow cotton shirtwaist dress that flattered her slim, petite figure. Her curly hair dried quickly in the August heat, falling softly around her small, pretty face, which had been freshly made up with rosy pink lipstick and dark brown mascara.

I had also had my Saturday soak in the galvanized tub, filled with warm water. Emerging from it freshly scrubbed and shampooed, I dressed in blue cotton pedal pushers and a white button-up shirt. When I walked outside where mama was playing with Bug, the leaves of a large maple tree fluttered, creating a gentle breeze that carried the readily-identifiable scent of Ivory soap with it. I inhaled deeply, enjoying the fragrance and the feeling of being 99 and 44/100 percent fresh and clean. This was the way I wanted to smell every day of my life.

"Darla Mae, I need for you to stay here and take care of Bug while I run to the store to pick up some things we need for tonight. Your daddy and Ben are down in the bottoms cutting some saplings to use for roasting the weenies. They ought to be back to the house before long." Mama caught Bug's exploring fingers before he could grab a button on her dress. "Bug needs to take a nap so he won't be fussy later."

"Bug always needs something," I muttered to myself. "Mama always needs me to do something, too." If mama heard me, she didn't say anything.

I was really disappointed that I wasn't going to the store with her. Now I was all dressed up with no place to go. Like many other times recently, this wasn't fair. That's how I felt for several moments, but then I thought about how much I enjoyed having some time all by myself. Maybe mama needed some time alone, too. She certainly didn't get much of it around here. Someday I'd be able to get all the alone time I wanted, but mama would always be stuck here on the farm. As much as I resented the way she treated me sometimes, I knew my life was going to be a lot better than hers had ever been. The least I could do was to be cooperative with her while I lived at home.

"OK, mama. I'll rock this little guy to sleep while you're gone." I took Bug from her, tossed a diaper over my shoulder, and held him close. He was cutting teeth, which meant that he was drooling all over the place all the time. I didn't want any of his saliva messing up my freshly-starched shirt. Bug gurgled and cooed as I sat down in a rocking chair where we would pass the time until mama returned. Kati had joined us, stretching her long, lean frame several times before curling up in a sunny spot on the porch.

Mama started the Dream Wagon, shifted into gear, and cautiously entered the dirt road that connected to Highway 41. Red dust followed her down the road and around the curve until she was out of sight. I was glad the wind didn't carry any of it over in my direction.

Mama had been gone only a few minutes when another cloud of dust moved in from the opposite direction, following an old white Cadillac that slowed, signaled, and turned into our driveway. Company! I could hardly contain my excitement and curiosity, along with a small measure of concern that it might be some strangers. Much to my relief, the person who got out of the car was someone I idolized—Jerry Adams.

"Jerry! When did you…? What brings you…?" I was so overjoyed at seeing him that I couldn't seem to string more than three words together. Tongue-tied idiot that I was, I couldn't even complete a sentence.

"Hey, Darla Mae. You're looking good." He flashed a brilliantly white smile at me. "To answer your questions, I'm home on leave for a few days before I go to Hawaii. Thought I'd stop by and see y'all before I leave here for a year." Mama had often said Jerry could charm apples right off the tree. I believed that he could, too.

Suddenly I was aware that I was staring at him, at his clean-shaven face, his incredible dark blue eyes, and his crew-cut blonde hair. He was my idea of handsome. Today he was neatly dressed in tight-fitting dungarees and a red-striped button-up shirt. My lips, my tongue, my mouth felt like they'd been glued together.

"Are your folks around?" he asked, glancing around the yard.

Finally, sensible words formed in my brain and fell from my lips. "Yeah, I mean yes. Daddy and Ben are in the bottoms cutting saplings for our weenie roast tonight. They ought to be home soon. Mama has gone to the store to get some weenies and stuff. She ought to be back in a few minutes, too." I laid sleepy little Bug in his playpen and offered Jerry a seat.

"Would you like a glass of sweet tea?" I asked while I was still standing.

"Sure, thanks. That'd be good."

I rushed into the house, nervously filled two glasses with ice cubes and poured tea over them, splashing some on the counter. Back outside, I sat the tea on a small metal table between his chair and mine.

"Thanks. Your mama makes the best tea of anybody I know. We sure don't get anything like it in the Navy. Our cooks make something they call tea, but it's more like stained water." Jerry took a long sip, shaking his glass a little, causing the ice cubes to clink against the sides.

"Mama is a good cook," I said. "I'm trying to learn as much as I can from her."

Jerry chuckled as if I had said something funny. "Darla Mae, you are all about learning. Are you still making all A's in school?"

"I did last year but every year gets harder," I said. "There seems to be more to learn and more work to do every year."

He agreed with me, "The lessons do get harder." We talked on about school for several minutes, chuckling about this and that. I felt like I was talking to Ben, like Jerry was an older brother to me, even though he was no kin at all.

At one point he asked, "Are you as good a student in Sunday school?

"No. We hardly ever go to Sunday school. But I do try to listen well in church, try to learn all I can there," I said.

"You know the lessons you learn in church can help you with all the other lessons you'll study in your life." Jerry's voice and expression had turned serious.

"How's that?" I asked.

"Well, if you believe in God and follow His commandments, you can't go wrong." He looked at me, a serious thoughtful expression in his eyes.

I looked away. Sister Sarah's words—"You'll do plenty that's wrong"—replayed in my mind. "I'm worried about that," I said, staring up at him again. He looked so good; if his face had been candy, I'd have taken a big bite.

"Worried about what?" Jerry asked. His eyes seemed to be searching my face for answers.

"Can I talk to you about something? Something that I don't want mama or daddy to know?" I know my voice sounded like I was pleading with him to say yes.

Jerry clamped his lips and scrunched his eyes together, causing a deep crease between his eyebrows. "Darla Mae, what on earth are you talking about?"

I gulped some iced tea, set the glass down with a thud, and mumbled, "Maybe I can't be good all my life. Maybe I can't follow the commandments every day, all the time. I've already broken three of them."

192

"You?" Jerry raised his eyebrows, plowing a deep furrow in his forehead. "You are such a little goody two-shoes." He must have realized that those words weren't exactly complimentary because he corrected himself. "I mean you are always considerate. You seem to be respectful of adults. You seem to care about other people. I can't imagine that you would ever do anything bad. It's just not in your nature. What makes you think otherwise?"

I told him about the pressure I was feeling to join a church. I told him about the little white lies, and the curiosity that I had about forbidden things, but I didn't mention fornicating because I didn't want him to know I was all that interested in something sinful. He listened intently, his facial expression changing as he thought about what I was saying. Finally I told him about the nightmares and how I couldn't tell mama and daddy about the dreams because they'd want to know what would make me dream such things. "I can't tell them. I just can't."

"First of all, I think you can stop worrying about what your friends are saying and doing. When I was your age, my friends were all joining churches, getting baptized, and all that. Part of me wanted to do the same thing, be just like them. It's hard to be different. The preacher up at the Baptist church had me believing that I was bound for hell if I didn't get my life right with Him that very day." He took a sip of tea and continued, "Well, you know me. I'm not like everybody else. I didn't get baptized until about six months ago at a military chapel."

"Really?" A stupid response on my part, but that's what came out of my mouth.

"Yes, really! I couldn't bring myself to do what everybody else was doing years ago, but one Sunday I was listening to the sermon when I got this strange feeling that God was talking to me. I got up and walked down that aisle to make my profession of faith as soon as the last hymn was being sung. It was the right thing to do and the right time to do it. While I can't tell you what to do, I can tell you that you'll know, Darla Mae, when it's the right time for you. In the meantime, just continue to be the good girl that you've always been." He glanced at me in a rather peculiar way before he said, "Unless, of course, you'd rather be a little devil for a while." He playfully slapped at my hand.

"I like doing devilish things—like dancing to rock 'n roll," I said as I wiggled in my chair.

"That wicked behavior is probably what is causing your nightmares," Jerry said, amusement tickling his lips.

"No. it isn't! Somebody else's wicked behavior is behind my dreams," I was about to tell Jerry Adams everything when I heard footsteps behind me.

"You are wicked," Ben said as he punched me in the shoulder with his clenched fist. I punched him back as best I could from a sitting position. Ben and I knew those were acts of affection, but daddy saw them otherwise.

"You've both got the devil in you. Now cut it out," daddy said before grabbing Jerry's right hand and pumping it hard. "Jerry Adams, it sure is good to see you. When did you get home? How long are you here? Can you stay for our weenie roast tonight?" Daddy had always liked Jerry and admired him for the way he'd taken charge of his life after his father died. If daddy could have adopted him, I believe he would have done it.

Jerry had stood up when he heard daddy's footsteps behind us. Now he was still gripping daddy's right hand in his, and smiling an electric smile while he said, "It's good to be back, Papa Walt. You know I consider this my second home. Couldn't get back in the area without coming by to see y'all."

Daddy beamed with mutual admiration.

"I'll be around for a week, and yes, I'd love to stay for a weenie roast. Haven't been to one of those in years. Can I help you do anything to get ready?" Jerry always seemed eager to be involved in whatever we were doing when he dropped by our house.

"Here's my knife," daddy said, offering a small knife that he'd just pulled from his pocket. "You can help Ben whittle those saplings to make poles for roasting the weenies while I get my Saturday afternoon shave." He stroked his grizzly three-day-old beard.

"Sure thing, Papa Walt," Jerry said as he clapped Ben's shoulder. They headed off to the tobacco barn with Ben hobbling on his crutches and talking a mile a minute. I heard the words "jet… broke sound barrier… want to be a pilot…" as they walked away.

Having time alone with Jerry Adams had made my day. I wanted to remember every word he had said, every sweet smile that had crossed his lips, and every token compliment he had paid me. Today I no longer felt like a lukewarm child. Instead I felt like a kettle of water, simmering with tiny bubbles beginning to break on the surface.

"Darla Mae, did you hear what I just asked you?" Daddy must have said something while I was staring at Ben and Jerry.

"Where's your mama?" he asked again.

I told him mama had gone to Russell's Store for some groceries, leaving me here to care for Bug. He rumpled my hair and said, "Don't know what we'd do without you to help with all the work around here, Darla Mae. You're gonna make a good wife for some man someday." His gray eyes sparked and twinkled.

"Maybe ten or twenty years from now. I've got a lot of living I want to do before I even think about getting married," I told him.

"That's my smart girl," daddy yelled from the side of the house where he'd picked up the galvanized aluminum bathtub. Inside he'd set his shave kit on the kitchen table, where he would slowly remove his whiskers one stroke at a time the way I'd seen him do all of my life. Afterwards he'd fill the tub with water and take his weekly bath, the one he took faithfully every Saturday, whether he needed it or not.

Preparations were complete with picnic tables in place, food covered against the inspection of curious flies, beverages iced in a peck bucket, and Bug's playpen safely set up near folding aluminum chairs which would be occupied by adults. Jerry, Ben, and I had taken turns cranking the ice cream churn until the liquid inside had frozen. Now the churn was packed in ice and wrapped with several layers of newspapers to keep it frozen until we ate it.

"Let's get some of these weenies roasted," daddy said as he passed a sapling pole to each of us. I threaded a fat, juicy hot dog over the pointed end far enough to keep it from falling off, then lowered it over hot coals in one of the barn's two fireboxes. Daddy had been adding more wood to the fire all day to increase the temperature inside the barn enough to finish curing the tobacco. Now there was a bed of hot coals that would cook a hot dog in a matter of minutes. I held my pole as close to the fire as I could get without touching it, turning it to brown the hot dog evenly. Heat caused the casing to expand and break open, allowing fat and moisture to drip on the hot coals with a hissing sound. Music to my ears. I could feel my stomach yearning for the first bite, but I continued to cook my hot dog until it was charred, leaving a crisp outer layer. This was my idea of a perfect, tasty treat.

Each of us took turns roasting the weenies just the way we liked them, talking all the time about cookouts we'd had in the past. The enticing aroma of roasted meat blended with the sweet, mellow fragrance of tobacco ripening in the barn.

"I wonder if city kids have any idea how much fun we have roasting weenies," I said to no one in particular.

"Oh, I 'spect they'd be surprised to know that you have any fun at all," daddy teased.

"I can tell you that some of the boys I have met in the Navy don't have a clue what life is like on a farm," Jerry said as he spread mustard over a bun, laid a nicely-browned hot dog on it, and covered it with coleslaw and onions. "They don't know what they're missing." He took a big bite and chewed it with relish, a look of pure pleasure spreading across his face.

"Looks like we might be the ones missing something," Cousin Charley said as he approached the barn.

"Hey, y'all!" Daddy walked over to greet Cousin Charley and Eva, who apparently had parked their car at the house and walked to the barn while we were so engaged in our chatter that we didn't hear them. Cousin

Charley shook daddy's hand and then nodded hellos to each of us.

"Come on over here and get yourself something to eat," mama motioned to Eva from her seat at the picnic table. "We're just getting started."

"Oh, we didn't come for supper. We just stopped by to give y'all some copies of the pictures we took on Sunday," Eva started to protest. She was wearing a nice rose print dress and short white heels, which suggested to me that they'd been somewhere else, or maybe they were on their way somewhere else and had just stopped by for a few minutes.

"Speak for yourself," Cousin Charley said as he eyed the table filled with food. "I haven't had a good barn-roasted hot dog in at least a year." Without regard for his navy dress pants and white short-sleeve shirt, Charley grabbed a pole, laced two hot dogs on it, and knelt in front of the firebox.

"Amazing, isn't it, that these saplings don't catch on fire," he said as he held the pole close to a mound of hot coals. Daddy squatted beside him, his bib overalls, plaid shirt, and scuffed clodhoppers in sharp contrast to his well-dressed cousin. "You know why, don't you?" daddy asked. They were soon into a semi-scientific discussion about how wet wood wouldn't burn right away. I tuned out.

Meanwhile mama had thrown one of Bug's blankets over a wooden bench to make a cleaner place for Eva to sit. "I wouldn't want splinters to pick your pretty new dress," she told Eva. I watched as Eva carefully stepped over the bench, seated herself, and began filling her plate. Mama was right about the need to make extras. We never knew who might drop by. Tonight I was happy to have the extra company who made our weenie roast an even more festive occasion.

"Do you know Jerry Adams?" mama asked Eva, who had looked quizzically at him. She proceeded to make the introductions.

"Aren't you Rachel Adams's son?" Eva asked as she continued to study his face.

"Yes, ma'am" Jerry answered politely.

"Rachel Simpson she was. I knew your mama when she lived on North Main Street. She and I went to school together at George Washington High. Then we worked together at Dan River Mills right after high school. I remember when your mama married Clifford Adams…" Eva went on connecting Jerry to people she knew, a familiar practice in our community, where just about everybody knew everybody and much of their business, even years after they'd moved away. Eva concluded with, "Well, how's your mama and 'em? I think about her real often, especially since your daddy died."

Jerry brought Eva up to date on all that was going on with him, his mother, his brothers, his sisters, and it seemed like half of his extended family. I sat quietly, enjoying my meal and the visual delight of this young man, who seemed so much a part of our family. He was so easy on the eyes; I could look at him forever. I could talk with him forever. I could follow his example, right up to the altar. He was definitely worthy of emulation, at least to me.

Emulation. Now that's another word Mrs. Rivers would be pleased to know that I remembered. She had often urged me to pay attention to my surroundings and to try to creatively describe them. As words played around in my head that night, I knew she would be pleased with where my mind was taking me.

I listened with curiosity and delight as the conversation ebbed and flowed around me, like tides in an ocean marsh whose rhythms are dictated by some unseen force of nature. When Bug whimpered, I picked him up and played patty-cake with him, still able to catch the gist of what the others were saying. Their voices broke the silence and serenity of the evening, creating a cacophony of sounds, sometimes soft and soothing, other times determined, persuasive, and electrifying. Combined, they exuded human warmth, companionship, and love.

Eva showed us the pictures that had been taken the previous Sunday. "Ben's got an eye for what makes a good photo," she said, patting Ben on the back. "I had copies made so that you all can have a set of these, too." She handed a packet to mama.

"Can you make that one of Darla Mae life-size?" Ben asked. "We could use it in the corn field for a scarecrow."

"No, we'd need your ugly mug for that," I said, immediately regretting how I had just reverted to being childish.

Daddy shot dirty looks at both of us, rose from his seat, ambled over to the barn door, and opened it cautiously. A blast of super-heated air escaped. "Whoa," daddy exclaimed as he backed away from the door for a moment. "It's hotter than forty hells in there!"

"Now, Walt, what would you know about how hot it is in hell?" mama asked with a voice that was harsh and chiding.

Cousin Charley's nose had twitched at the mention of that devilish place. He stared at daddy for a moment before saying, "Maybe you'd better let *me* go in to check the thermometer."

"Keep your seat. I've been curing tobacco for about twenty-five years now. I think I can handle a little heat." Daddy stepped inside the door, shone a flashlight on the thermometer, and immediately came outside, closing the barn door behind him.

"One hundred fifty degrees. That'll dry out the stems in a hurry. We'll be done with this barn of tobacco tomorrow," he announced with what appeared to be smug satisfaction before adding a few more logs to each firebox.

I walked over to roast another hot dog. There I watched flames leap from piles of hot coals onto the dried wood, igniting it almost instantly, causing it to crackle, charring it, and turning it to ashes in a matter of minutes. There was something disturbingly familiar about what was taking place inside this firebox. Earlier I had found the fire to be a thing of warmth, beauty, and a joy to behold. The red, yellow, and blue flames that danced and played among the embers mesmerized me. Now I saw that the fire consumed everything in its path, condemning layers of once healthy trees to eternal nothingness. My thoughts were rampant, but I didn't verbalize them.

Eva must have noticed a change in my expression as I gazed at that inferno, because she came over and whispered in my ear, "Are you OK?"

Her soft blue eyes met mine in the fading sunset, conveying so much understanding that I forced a thin smile, and whispered back, "Yeah. Yes, I'm fine." I was telling the truth. I was fine, but not nearly as fine as I was going to be the next day. Deep inside I knew that the next day would be the perfect time for me to get my life right with God.

❧

Daddy was sitting on an armless wooden bench, his back erect, legs apart, a guitar suspended by a wide strap around his neck. He twisted the tuning knobs and strummed with his right hand, while running his calloused fingers up and down the neck. Satisfied at last that he'd tuned the guitar the way he wanted, daddy started to play a song Jimmie Davis made famous in the 1940's, "You Are My Sunshine."

Jerry retrieved a guitar from his car and was soon playing along with daddy, stopping and starting again as they tried to remember the words and tunes to some country hits. Cousin Charley hummed along until they sang something familiar before joining in with his strong baritone voice. Mama, Eva, and I forgot about our lack of talent and joined right in, singing out of tune and off key about half the time, but being tone deaf, we didn't know the difference.

"What did you do with the money mama gave you?" Ben asked me.

"What money?" I didn't know what he was talking about.

"The money mama gave you for voice lessons," Ben said, thumping me on the shoulder with his index finger as he walked by. I smiled a loving smile at him and thought to myself, "I'm going to kill you with kindness." Then I held my nose and purposefully sang with a nasal twang. Both of us laughed, as did everyone else.

An old car rumbled down the road with the radio blaring bluegrass music through its open windows. "Sweet Sue," daddy said. "She's back living with Trickem, since they put her mama in a nursing home. He told me the other day she was coming back. Said he'd told her he had quit drinking and that he was going to start going to church every Sunday and try to be the man he ought to be."

"She must love that ole rascal to be willing to take him back after all they've been through," mama said. "I hope they make a go of it this time."

"So do I," Cousin Charley chimed in. "It's about time for that old boy to grow up."

"I always thought he had better sense than he used most of the time. Then I saw him picking yellow jackets off of Ben and I knew his brain was addled. But what he did may have saved Ben's life. I can't thank him enough. I can never give him enough money to repay him for that," daddy said, his eyes locked on Ben.

In the distance a mourning dove called its sad refrain. A gentle breeze kept us cool and the mosquitoes at bay. Overhead a bright, full moon lit the night sky, casting long shadows over everything in sight. Soon the sky was filled with thousands of stars, glittering like tiny light bulbs on black velvet. I could get lost, staring into them now and wondering what it might be like to fly among them some-day. Everything seemed to be right in my tiny world here on planet earth. My friendship with Latisha was cemented for the future. My convictions about the merits of all races were established. My belief that there is some good in all people was borne out by the neighborhood rascal, and I knew what I was going to do at church the next day. I wanted this perfect evening to last all night.

When daddy finished one song, I'd try to think of another one for him to play. He eventually played one he'd written himself, "She's My Curly-Headed Alene," a tribute to my mother. Mama busied herself with bouncing Bug on her knee, avoiding daddy's almost liquid eyes.

At ten o'clock Cousin Charley stood, turned to Eva and said, "Guess we'd better get on home. One of us has to work tomorrow." He grinned, a toothy grin that made his long thin face look almost round. "Will we see y'all in church in the morning?" he asked, looking at daddy for confirmation.

Mama answered immediately. "No, we are going to Healing Waters tomorrow."

I saw daddy's lips tighten, like he was trying not to let anybody know how he felt about mama's answer. He locked eyes with her for an instant, and then turned away.

"Healing Waters! Good," I thought. "That's where I would rather get baptized."

Mama explained, "They're having a group of gospel singers who have come all the way from Mississippi to present a special program. The Next of Kin, I think they're called."

"I've heard of them," Eva said. "They're supposed to be right good." She helped mama cover the leftovers and stack empty bowls.

"Well, I met two of them—sisters—down at Russell's Store today. There is a brother who sings with them, too, and other members of their family join in sometimes. They were real friendly. Said they've traveled around the country a lot. They're staying with some of the church members tonight since there aren't any hotels closer than Danville." Mama talked as she picked up paper plates, napkins, and cups to toss in the fire.

"Y'all ought to have good attendance tomorrow," Eva noted.

"I expect so. Reverend Hardshell apparently told the congregation last Sunday that he wants all the members there to fill up the church," mama said. She turned to look at Cousin Charley. "I'm sorry we can't be in both places at the same time."

"That's alright, Alene. So long as you are in church somewhere. Can't say that I blame Reverend Hardshell for wanting a crowd. Just don't give him all your money," Cousin Charley said with a grin.

"No danger of that happening," daddy assured him. He turned one pants pocket inside out and caught three dimes and two pennies, much to our amusement.

We said our farewells to Cousin Charley and Eva, agreeing to see them again in a couple of weeks. Jerry departed shortly afterwards with a promise to write to us from Hawaii. He hugged mama, shook hands with daddy, gave Ben a slap on the shoulder, and took my hand for one brief moment, then winked at me while saying, "Be good!"

I floated on back to the house, carrying a basket of leftover food, dishes, and serving spoons, all the while thinking about how very special this evening had been. The next day would be an even more significant day in my life.

Sleep came that night only after I had tossed and turned for several hours, trying to get my brain to shut up and my heart to slow its unusually rapid beat. Something was happening inside me that I couldn't seem to control. Soon I would turn everything over to God and see where he would lead me.

Chapter 21

Sunday morning dawned bright and sunny, but dark, ominous clouds started to roll in from the west as we drove to Healing Waters Gospel Church in the community of Stillwater, about five miles from our home. My family all seemed to be in a good mood that morning, chatting about the previous night's weenie roast, the day's chores, the need for rain, and other such topics. Nothing intellectually stimulating. Nothing earth shattering. Just the ordinary daily sharing of thoughts and observations.

At the large, white, clapboarded church I hopped out of the Dream Wagon and ran over to join a cluster of girls standing under the canopy of a large old maple tree. Some of them were true friends, people who knew everything about me and still liked me, while some were just friendly acquaintances. A few were obnoxious enemies. One skinny girl with long, auburn hair, a thin face, and pointy nose glared at me and said, "Well, look who's here. Darla Mae Deacons. You've been away so long; we thought you'd joined those colored holy rollers at the AME church."

Her high, shrill voice and mention of "holy rollers" caught the attention of the other girls, who stopped their conversations to hear my reply. I wanted to slap that smug smirk right off her ugly face. Instead, remembering advice Mrs. Rivers had given me, I took a deep breath, smiled my most ingratiating smile at her and said, "It's good to see you too, Janice."

She squinted at me through half-shut hazel eyes, rolled out her pouty lips and shrugged her bony shoulders, then walked away with a couple of like-minded girls. None of them did well in school. I knew they resented me because I made good grades, which they attributed to my being the teacher's pet. They didn't approve of my friendship with Latisha. "Let them say what they want, think what they want, and do what they want. I will not let them ruin this special day for me," I thought as I turned to the friends standing next to me.

A chubby blonde with a freckled face whispered, "Good comeback, Darla Mae."

Another one of my friends, a really pretty girl with black hair and violet eyes, nodded her head ever so slightly. "What was that all about anyway?" she asked.

"Jealousy. She's been jealous of me since first grade," I said, rocking back and forth on white princess heels that gripped my summer feet like a vise. "And the fact that I haven't been 'saved' yet gives her something to feel superior about." I hoisted my nose in the air, rolled my eyes, and tried to mimic her snootiness.

"You haven't joined church yet? You're almost twelve. What are you waiting for?" another girl asked, her face contorted in disbelief.

"The right time," I said, while smiling into her green eyes.

Church bells began to peal, announcing the time to gather in the sanctuary for the start of the day's worship service. We filtered in and scattered to find our parents. Most of them held the belief that worship was a family affair, that their children would benefit the most from the services if they were seated directly beside their moms and dads.

Ben soon joined my parents, Bug, and me on a pew about five rows from the back of the sanctuary. I settled myself on the hard, oak bench and said a silent prayer that we'd get to stand up enough that my bony little butt wouldn't get achy before the service was over. Immediately I knew that this was a stupid prayer and one that God wouldn't want to hear. Even so, I hoped that someday we would have a nice, thick cushion on the pews, like the ones I had seen in some city churches.

The congregation was still buzzing about the special program of music today as they chose seats, many going to their usual pew, stopping to greet others around them. A light breeze drifted through open windows, bringing some relief in a room that was growing warmer with each additional person. Among the last to enter the church was an elderly couple who hurried down the long red carpeted aisle, tapping their canes as they went all the way to the front row.

While waiting for the timeless rituals which would begin the day's service, I examined my family, noting that daddy had worn a pair of brown dress pants, a crisply-starched white short- sleeved shirt, and a multi-colored "choke strap," daddy's name for a necktie. He hated ties almost as much as he hated wearing a belt, which he always called a bellyband. This morning, I thought he looked really good. Clean, freshly shaved, nicely dressed.

Daddy glanced at me and winked. I had told him about my desire to join church today while we were taking care of the morning chores. He stared off in the distance for a moment or two before saying, "Darla Mae, I know this is something that seems to be real important to you right now. You know I wish you would wait until you are older, until you really understand what you are getting into, but I am not going to stand in your way. What kind of father would I be to tell you that you couldn't join a church?"

"Thanks, daddy. The time just seems right to me. Jerry Adams said it would. I'm a little worried though about what mama will say."

"You'd better tell her about your plans," daddy said, his index finger pointed at me, emphasizing each word.

"OK, I will. I'll tell her before the service starts." I turned and rushed up the hill toward the house before daddy could see my chin twitching, the way it always did when I told a lie. There was no way I was going to tell mama I planned to join church today. She might forbid me to do it since she was so adamant that I must be older before I made that kind of commitment. What could she do once I started down that aisle? Reach out and grab me? I didn't think so. I thought she would be too embarrassed to try to stop me.

My thoughts were tumbling around in my head like sand in a cement mixer as I scanned the crowd and made mental note of who was present. I spotted Trickem and Sweet Sue sitting on the opposite side of the church. I wondered if they might rededicate their lives to Christ today. If they did, I wouldn't be standing up there at that altar all by myself.

I shifted my glance to mama, whose light, silky hair was in strong contrast to her navy jewel-necked short-sleeved dress, one of two in her "Sunday-go-to-meeting" wardrobe. Ben was also neatly groomed today. Brylcream held brown wavy hair in place around his slender, deeply tanned face, which was beginning to sprout fine light hair. He tugged at tan pants that were getting too tight in the waist and too short at the ankles. A turquoise plaid shirt, unbuttoned at the neck, showed off a developing Adam's apple. Mama had dressed Bug in a pair of red shorts and a striped shirt that she had recently made, complaining all the time about how fast he was outgrowing all of his clothes. We may not get to church every Sunday, but when we go, we are pretty well turned-out for poor people, I thought. Then I smoothed the full-gathered skirt of my homemade yellow cotton dress and tried to flatten the puffy crinolines peeking from underneath it. This morning I sat up straight, determined to hear every word of the day's service.

Two young male acolytes, attired in red and white gowns, sauntered to the front of the church to light two tall candles which flanked the altar table, while the pianist played and the choir sang "Open My Eyes, That I May See." I recalled the words. I loved the part about having a key put in my hands that would set me free. Yes, I was ready to see God's will for me. "Open my eyes, illumine me, Spirit divine!" I sang with all the enthusiasm I could muster.

Perfectly chosen, just for me, just for today, it seemed.

Brother Hendricks, the lay minister, a rotund man with a broad face and balding head who appeared to be older than dirt (at least sixty) welcomed everybody in a nervous voice, one of almost forced cheerfulness. He gave a brief opening prayer, then asked us to stand and sing "Gloria Patri," before announcing the morning's special program of gospel music by The Next of Kin from Tupelo, Mississippi.

When he said Tupelo, my mind wandered off again. Wasn't that where Elvis was born? I tried to remember. I wondered if they knew him. Wouldn't that be awesome? I thought. Maybe they will tell us that he sang with them in Sunday school before moving to Memphis. I conjured up an image of Elvis as a little boy, playing a guitar and singing hymns. "Stop," I had to tell myself. "Get your mind back on the service, especially this morning."

The trio took their places near the altar, signaled to the pianist to begin, and sang "How Great Thou Art" loudly, clearly, beautifully. I sat there enchanted by the harmonious blending of their voices singing praises to God. Their brown eyes sparkled; their faces glowed as if illuminated from within, much like stained glass windows, revealing their true beauty when the light shines through them at night. I wondered if this was what happened to people who were truly committed to loving God, and to leaving the sinful life behind. The fact that these people had traveled all this way to sing to us really impressed me. So did their appearance. The women looked almost angelic in beautiful white taffeta chemise-style dresses, their long copper-colored hair hanging in curls around their shoulders.

At one point, the male member of the trio, a slender fellow with jet-black hair, asked us to stand and sing

"Standing on the Promises" with them. I was so grateful to them, not just for giving me a chance to relieve my aching butt, but also for allowing me to sing along, something that I had wanted to do from the very beginning, whenever they sang something I knew. Ben and I tried to out-sing each other.

In the middle of their program, Brother Hendricks prayed a lengthy prayer, followed by the passing of two collection plates, one for the Sunday offering to the church and another for a "love" offering for The Next of Kin. I watched as daddy pulled his thin well-worn wallet from his pocket. I knew that this part of the service always made him uncomfortable, as it did many of the farmers in attendance. They were embarrassed, knowing that the church expected them to tithe and make additional contributions to any special offerings. They also knew, as did their children, that another month would pass before the tobacco markets opened, allowing them to sell their crops and replenish the bank accounts from which they would pay their bills for the next year. August was a month of scrimping, saving, and stretching every dollar as far as it would go. Daddy hung his head, looked in the wallet again, and extracted two bills that he folded into fourths, concealing the denominations. He grimaced as he put one in each plate. Other men on our pew passed both plates without acknowledgement.

Both collection plates ended up at the back of the church, where two of the ushers were responsible for counting the love offering and putting it in an envelope which would be handed to the singers on their way out of the church. Two other ushers, who performed their duties with the precision of well-trained military men, carried the regular offering to the altar. When the pianist began to play, we stood and sang our words of praise.

After the doxology, The Next of Kin began to perform again—familiar hymns and some that sounded like a blend of bluegrass and gospel. Mama and daddy seemed to be enjoying the program as much as I was. They'd glance my way occasionally, nod their heads, and smile. Ben silently mouthed the words to the songs he knew, lightly punching me with his elbow from time to time, as if to say "We could be singing that one." Bug chewed on his teething ring, fretting occasionally, but totally oblivious to all that was going on around him.

About two-thirds of the way through the service, my mind strayed from the singing to take note of Reverend Hardshell's absence. I thought it strange, and an out and out shame that he was missing such an outstanding morning of worship. Maybe he was at a conference, I thought, or maybe he was on vacation, since his wife and children were not there either. Those thoughts were brushed aside as I forced myself to pay attention.

Forty-five minutes into the service, The Next of Kin announced their closing song and asked us to stand and sing with them "Gi'Me That Ole Time Religion." Everybody who was able stood and sang loudly along with them.

"It was good enough for grandma. It was good enough for grandpa. Gi'me that ole time religion." We clapped our hands, swayed with the music, and belted out the words. "Oh, yes, this is good enough for me," I thought, as I lustily sang along with the rest of the congregation. Everything about this morning just felt so right to me.

The Next of Kin finished with a rousing round of applause, something quite unusual in this conservative country church. We continued to applaud, hoping that they'd sing at least one more for us, but the male singer said, "We'd love to stay here and sing for y'all the rest of the day, but we've got to get to Spartanburg, South Carolina, by seven o'clock tonight. Y'all pray for a safe journey for us and until next time: May "God Be with You 'Til We Meet Again."

They sang that song as they walked to the back of the church and out the door, amid the clapping hands, smiling faces, and nodding heads of the congregation. We heard the engine of their car start and the wheels crunch on loose gravel as they drove away.

If only we could have left with them, this day would have been glorious in every way, even if I had to wait another week to make my profession of faith. What happened next will forever be etched in my memory.

Brother Hendricks' usually jovial face transformed from delighted animation to mortuary seriousness. He paused at the altar, surveyed the worshipers, wiped perspiration from his brow with a large white handkerchief, and shuffled to his right, then to his left, jostling his rotund girth.

When he finally spoke, his voice cracked, as if he had been under great emotional strain. "Christian friends, we have some business to take care of before y'all leave here today."

"Yes," I thought. "You've got to have your hymn of invitation so that I can make my public profession of faith. But that is a joyous moment. Why are you sounding like the bearer of bad news?" I wondered. Of course, he had no way of knowing that I wanted to dedicate my life to Christ that day.

"Some of you may have wondered why I am here today instead of Reverend Hardshell. Well, I'm here because he asked me to lead today's service. I'll be here next week and for as long as I'm needed after that. Reverend Hardshell will tell you why." Brother Hendricks shuffled over to the door that led to the minister's office, knocked on it, and waited for Reverend Hardshell to emerge. Such quiet fell over the congregation that one could have heard a stomach growl three pews away. All eyes were on the altar.

Reverend Hardshell staggered out and tearfully approached the altar where he knelt and prayed before turning to speak to the congregation. His clothes were as wrinkled as if he'd slept in them. His hair was rumpled, and he had a two-day growth of beard. A man whose usually brilliant smile greeted the faithful now bit his trembling lips. I stole a glance at mama whose tight face was trying to hold back tears.

"Members of Healing Waters Gospel Church, I come to you today with the heaviest heart that I have ever known." He paused. We waited silently, respectfully. "My wife has left me. She's taken the children and gone to live with her mother in Missouri." He sobbed into his handkerchief. An audible gasp went up from some in the congregation.

"It's all my fault," he continued in a halting, blubbering manner. "I am guilty—guilty of the sins I have so often preached against here from this very pulpit." He hung his head and cried, muttering these words: "Guilty of adultery. Adultery with not one, but with several women in this community. Guilty of fornication. Guilty of sins of the flesh. Guilty of fathering at least one child by someone other than my wife."

Almost simultaneously three babies started to cry—to scream—as if they'd been pinched. Bug was one of them. Mama, ashen-faced, immediately took him outside, as did the other two mothers, who were seated a few rows ahead of us. Three other women herded their young children out of the church. Everyone else turned, stared, and followed these women out the church, with eyes that rolled with suspicion and condemnation.

I looked at daddy, whose eyes were blazing the way they did when he was trying to burn a hole in my brain, only this time his scorching stare was focused on Reverend Hardshell. Daddy's arms were crossed, his fists clenched. He was muttering, tight-jawed, under his breath. I heard the words "son of a gun." Daddy must have suspected what he hoped no one would ever confirm. I joined daddy in glaring at Reverend Hardshell, furious beyond description, livid, ready to explode.

Ben looked perplexed, his eyes rolling from side to side, trying to take in all the commotion that was going on around us. Within seconds, many men, women, and children had joined the exodus from the church. Some were holding their hands over their ears as if they could blot out the sinfulness of what they were hearing.

My nimble mind had picked up on the word "adultery" and I instinctively knew now what it meant. I missed some of Reverend Hardshell's words after that, catching only phrases: "God forgive me... going back to Georgia... so sorry for all the harm I've done here... lost everything... burn in hell... Oh, God, forgive me! Forgive me!"

All six feet four inches of his athletic body crumpled to the floor, the sobbing mass of a sinful man.

Brother Hendricks saw the congregation's response and made no effort to regain control nor conclude the service in any way. Some people had made their way to the front of the church where they knelt to pray while others fled through side doors. All around me faces reflected shock, horror, anguish, and revulsion. Mouths uttered words never used in church. Reverend Hardshell remained on the floor, sobbing more pitifully than anything I'd ever heard, even at funerals.

I sat there, fixated on the sight of this minister who'd fallen from grace, in such a state of shock that Ben had to shake me out of my stupor. "Come on, let's get out of this crazy place," he said as he tugged on my arm. "Daddy's already on his way to the car." I glanced around and saw him at the back of the church mumbling to Trickem.

"Just a minute," I said, not knowing what to do now that the day, which had started out to be so special, had come to such a disturbing end. Profoundly disappointed, my blood boiled inside my pounding heart as my mind raced through a jumble of emotions sharp as a razor's edge—rage, rancor, resentment, and disillusionment among them. This was supposed to have been my special day. Now this preacher, this "burn in hell" preacher, whose words had traumatized my dreams, had ruined it for me.

I stared at the life-size portrait of Christ behind the pulpit for what seemed like an hour. His serious eyes seemed to stare back at me, prodding me to remember his teachings. Eventually, I recalled what he had done on Calvary's cross and what he had said of his enemies.

Before we walked out of the church, I bowed my head and offered up a silent prayer, one that I was certain Cousin Charley, Eva, and Jerry Adams would have had me to pray: "Dear God, I came prepared to give my life to you today. I still want to try to live a righteous life, and I need your guidance to do that. Please help me to understand why good people do bad things. Help me to forgive them. And please, dear God, forgive me for all my wrong doings today and always. Amen."

I flicked tears away from my eyes, took a quick glance at an altar I knew I would not see again for a very long time, and then walked out of the church, believing I had established that *serious* commitment with God.

Chapter 22

Storm clouds that had gathered all morning finally opened up on our drive home, sending a torrent of water beating against the Dream Wagon. Inside the car, the climate was icy. None of us seemed to be able to utter a word. The whine of the engine, the hum of tires on wet pavement, and the harsh plop-plop of the rain was all that broke the silence the entire way home. Even Bug sat still.

When he stopped in the driveway, daddy turned to Ben and me and said, "Y'all change clothes and get yourself a sandwich or something. Take it on outside to eat it. Me and your mama got some talking to do."

We complied with his wishes as quickly as we could, eager to escape the tension that laid like a heavy, wet blanket over us. In the treehouse, we settled ourselves on the floor, sandwiches and sweet tea in our hands, and ate in silence as rain continued to tap against the roof. Ben finally asked, "What do you think they are talking about?"

This question was the opening I needed to tell Ben everything I had wanted to tell him for months. Between sobs and sniffles, I told him about what I'd seen almost two years before, what I'd heard that day at Lois' house, what I'd dreamed about more times than I could remember.

"Now, today, I was finally going to join that church, get baptized, and get my life right with God. That preacher ruined it all for me! I hate him. I hate mama." I dripped tears all over my clean shirt. Kati had given up on trying to catch them and had curled up on her blanket next to me.

Ben handed me a ragged handkerchief that he'd found in a corner of the treehouse. His eyes full of pity, he said, "Sis, there'll be plenty of opportunities for you to join a church in the years ahead. Maybe you'll find a different church. Maybe you'll decide to join Cousin Charley's church where you and Sister Sarah can sing together in the choir. Maybe by that time, I'll make the walk to the altar with you."

"Hmmph," I muttered. We sat there for several minutes, not talking, just keeping each other company. Finally I said, "I don't know what's going to happen now. Don't know what mama and daddy are going to do. I hope he doesn't kill her."

"Darla Mae, you know daddy better than that. He would never hurt anybody. Not bad, anyway." We stayed in the tree house for what seemed like hours, talking about all sorts of things. Finally, I was able to stop crying long enough to laugh at something Ben had said.

"Let's go back to the house," I suggested after I had dried my eyes.

"I'll race you," Ben said, when he reached the bottom of the tree house ladder. We ran, lickety-split through the puddles, charging through the back door with muddy feet.

Mama and daddy seemed so lost in their own thoughts that they hardly noticed us. It was not until we stomped upstairs that daddy called to us, "Y'all come back down here. We need to talk about all that's happened today." When we got back to the kitchen he was holding his head in his hands, like he had a really bad headache.

Ben and I took our seats at the table and waited for one of them to speak. Moments passed while mama sniffled and wiped away tears. Daddy mumbled something to himself that sounded like he was praying. I heard, "Lord, help me to find the right words."

Finally he looked up, made eye contact with Ben and me, and spoke. "That was an awful scene at church this morning—quite a scandal that was revealed. Everybody is going to think your mama was one of the women involved with that man. Y'all are old enough to know the truth, so I'm just going to tell it." He coughed a few times like he was trying to clear a path for the words he was about to say.

"She was one of Hardshell's women. *Was*. Remember that word—*was*—isn't anymore. I found out about it when we were going through some bad times a little over a year ago." Daddy's face contorted; his voice cracked as he choked back tears.

"We hoped nobody else would ever find out," mama blubbered. The sorrow in mama's eyes and on her face was greater than Aunt Essie's had been at Uncle Travis' funeral.

Had I heard daddy right? A little over a year ago? Daddy knew about mama and that man? He didn't have to hear about it from me. I sat there stunned that daddy knew what I had tried to keep a secret until this very day. I took a deep, lung-filling breath. Relief washed over me like water flowing over a dam. "Thank you, Lord," I said silently. I exchanged glances with Ben, glad that I had told him what I had seen, what I had heard all those months ago.

Daddy coughed a couple more times, regained his composure, and continued, "Your mama and me were going to get a divorce. The more we thought about it and the more we talked about it, the more we realized that we loved each other too much to call it quits. We loved y'all too much to break up our family. By that time, Bug was on the way, so there was one more reason to stay together, to work things out." He reached over, took mama's left hand in his, and rubbed the simple gold band that circled her finger.

"Now we may have to live with the scandal for a while, but with other women leaving the church at the same time, there will be some others for people to gossip about. Don't y'all get caught up in it. If anyone asks why your mama was one of the first women to walk out of the service, tell them it was because Bug was crying. That's the truth."

Again, Ben and I exchanged glances which included weak smiles. Mama found her voice, "I made a really bad mistake. I committed a terrible sin. I am so sorry," mama said between sobs. "I never meant to hurt your daddy like I did. If I had thought any of this would ever come out in public, I would never have got involved with that man. I ought to have known that nothing stays a secret forever. Sooner or later, your sins will find you out." She stopped talking long enough to take care of her sniffles. "I'm so thankful I have a loving husband and a loving God who forgave me."

Her words took me back to the prayer I had prayed right before I left the church. Immediately, my heart softened as if God was speaking to me. Mama looked so pitiful, I felt sorry for her, wanted to do something to help her feel better. I walked around the table, wrapped my arms around her shoulders, gave her a hug, and said, "Mama, I forgive you, too." She hugged me back, a warm affectionate hug that left me misty-eyed again. I turned to my father, hugged him, and said "I love you, Daddy." His eyes reflected more love than I had ever known.

Light suddenly flooded the kitchen, as the sun emerged from behind clouds that were quickly dispersing. Outside, the leaves of all the plants and trees shimmered, breathing easier now that the dust had been washed away. Inside it seemed that our family had been cleansed and renewed by the events of the day, too.

Ben had given both parents a quick hug before rescuing Bug from his crib, where he had awakened, wet and crying. "Some mundane aspects of life never change," I said to myself, as I took care of Bug's needs. Later on the front porch, I held him close, grateful for his presence in our family.

That night, I said my prayers, gave thanks that our family was going to stay together, that our secrets had been revealed. I felt closer to God and closer to Ben than ever. When I closed my eyes, I knew that a peaceful sleep would come at last.

Acknowledgements

Many people deserve thanks for their contributions to the development of this novel, starting with my writer friends in Mount Pleasant, South Carolina. The late Irene Lofton taught the first writing class that I ever took, inspiring me instantly with words that were meant to unleash creativity. Mary Olimpio, Gail Costa, Amy Hardee, Arlene Sopa, Karen Durand, and others in the 5W's writing group provided constant encouragement and positive feedback.

Thank you to author and teacher, Maudy Benz, for asking students in a creative writing class at Durham Tech to work on a longer project, which was the beginning of this book. Thanks also to the other students in that class for your critical evaluations. To Debra Rosenstein, a huge thank you and lots of hugs for reminding me of the sights, sounds, and smells of the 1950's. Attending the North Carolina Writer's Network conferences and lunching together in Hillsborough made the process of writing a novel very enjoyable.

To my friend, Bev Tiller, thank you for laughing in all the right places when you read selected chapters. To my friend, Micki Pugh, thank you for your continued interest in this book and for your insightful questions that prompted reconsideration of some aspects.

Thanks to my former Duke University OLLI classmates for your honest, succinct feedback of some of my other writing, which resulted in the formation of the Monday writing group. To those group members: Betty Hopkins, Muki Fairchild, Joan Tetel Hanks, Art Mella, Ralph Heinz, and Bob Wilkinson, an enormous thank you for being incredibly patient as you read this work over an eighteen-month period, provided lots of constructive criticism, and always supported my endeavors in getting this work published. I know a few of you wanted action-packed car chase scenes and other thriller concepts written into the story. Sorry I couldn't accommodate you!

I would never have reached this point without the help of author, mentor, and friend, Erika Karres, who read the novel, asked the right questions, offered excellent suggestions, and pushed me when I needed to do more. Thank you, Erika, from the bottom of my heart.

To my deceased mother, Ethel Kirks, I owe a debt of gratitude. When I was growing up, she always said, "Learn to push a pencil." She believed that writing was a skill that could take me off the farm and into a better life. While I was writing this book, she helped me to establish a sense of time and place during our conversations about what church was like in the 1950's.

To my dear husband, Jerry, thank you for listening when I needed to talk about this book and for offering technical assistance and encouragement throughout the process. I love you!

To all my readers, hugs and thanks for taking a chance on the debut novel of an unknown writer. I hope that you enjoy the book and find yourselves remembering the '50's and thinking about your own experiences of that era, if you were around then. To all the young readers, I urge you to think about and talk about how your own experiences with race, religion, truth, and commitment compare with Darla Mae's.

Youth Readers Discussion Guide

Commitment

1. Choose your favorite three characters in this book. Describe them in terms of their physical characteristics and their personality traits. Tell why you liked them.

2. Were there any characters you didn't like? Who were they? What did you dislike about them?

3. Darla Mae seems to have trouble paying attention at times, yet she picks up on vocabulary, grammar, and dialect. In quoting others, she includes their errors. Which errors bothered you the most? How would you correct them?

4. How did Darla Mae's summer activities compare with the way you spent this past summer?

5. Have you ever spent a week or more on a farm? If so, where? How did your experience differ from the days that Darla Mae tells about in this story?

6. Why does Darla Mae feel such a strong need to get her life right with God? Which of the factors influencing her need are the same factors influencing the needs of young people today?

7. What do you think Darla Mae's dreams are really about? What do you think she could have or should have done about them?

8. Several people influenced Darla Mae's thinking and commitment. Who do you think influenced her the most and how?

9. From the beginning, Darla Mae is challenging the racial practices of her day. Discuss ways in which these practices have changed. Have any stayed the same? If so, which ones? Why do think those remain the same as they were in 1958?

10. Young people sometimes say they would rather be spanked than lectured when they do something wrong. Darla Mae's parents used several different methods of discipline in this story. Which one do you think was most effective and why?

11. Darla Mae loves words, particularly those taught by Mrs. Rivers. Identify and define five of them.

12. When is a person actually "saved"? What part does baptism actually play in a person's salvation?

13. Who else had made a commitment that influenced the outcome of this story? What evidence do you have of this commitment?

14. The author told this story in first person, using the perspective of Darla Mae. How would the story have been different if it had been told from the perspective of one of the other characters? From the third person, omnipotent perspective?

15. If you could write a sequel to *Commitment*, what would you want Darla Mae to do in your story?

Mature Readers Discussion Guide

Commitment

1. Darla Mae witnessed a very disturbing scene and later overheard a disturbing conversation. She chose to keep both a secret. Was this the right thing to do? Justify your answer.

2. Darla Mae's family attended the funeral of a colored man in 1958. Would your family have done that? What factors would have influenced that decision?

3. From the beginning, Darla Mae is challenging the racial practices of her time. Discuss ways in which these practices have changed. Have any stayed the same? If so, which ones? Why do you think they have stayed the same as they were in 1958?

4. Darla Mae's friendship with Latisha seems to portend societal changes to come. Discuss Darla Mae's relationship with Latisha and how they complemented each other.

5. Discuss ways in which Darla Mae's everyday life in 1958 compared with yours. If you were not around in 1958, discuss the ways your life was different when you were between ten and twelve years old.

6. A person's religious beliefs are greatly influenced by their parents' beliefs. Discuss your agreement or disagreement with this statement. Which parent had the greatest influence on Darla Mae's beliefs and how?

7. Was Darla Mae "saved" when she left church on that memorable Sunday in August of 1958? If not, when does a person's salvation actually occur?

8. Darla Mae's parents used several different methods of discipline in this story, including a "whipping." Which do you think was most effective and why?

9. While growing up we learn to make and keep commitments. Who do you think was the most "committed" person in this story and why? Explain how that commitment influenced the outcome of the story.

10. Which elements in this book are typically found in southern literature?

11. Did the use of flash-backs accelerate or impede the reader of this book? Explain your answer.

12. If you could rewrite the ending or write a sequel to this book, what would you want to see happen in it?

About the Author:

Photo by Amy Stearn

Phyllis Kirks Crabb lives in Durham, NC, with her husband and their two Siamese cats. She earned her undergraduate and graduate degrees in education and counseling from Radford College (now Radford University). After teaching for nine years and counseling for twenty-one in Virginia's public schools, she retired to Mt. Pleasant, SC, where she studied creative writing and joined a writers' group, which fostered her love of writing. In Durham, she pursued further writing experiences through Duke University's Osher Lifelong Learning Institute, the University of North Carolina's Community Classroom Series, and Durham Technical Community College's summer program. This, her debut novel, evolved from those experiences.

Born and raised in rural southern Virginia, Phyllis experienced first-hand the farm life of the 1950's, enabling her to bring the fictional community of McKenzie, and its lovable, believable, characters, amazingly to life. All can sympathize with Darla Mae as she wrestles with her out-sized dilemmas and dreams en route to making her momentous, serious commitment.

CPSIA information can be obtained
at www.ICGtesting.com
Printed in the USA
FFOW03n1350300315
12208FF